Bloodsong

Bloodsong

AND OTHER STORIES
OF SOUTH AFRICA

Ernst
Havemann

Houghton Mifflin Company

BOSTON

1987

A RICHARD TODD BOOK

Library of Congress Cataloging-in-Publication Data

Havemann, Ernst.
Bloodsong and other stories of South Africa.

"A Richard Todd book" — T.p. verso.
1. South Africa — Fiction. I. Title.
PR9199.3.H3642B56 1987   813'.54   86-27342
ISBN 0-395-43296-0

Printed in the United States of America

Q 10 9 8 7 6 5 4 3 2 1

Several of the stories in this collection have appeared, in slightly different form, elsewhere: "A Farm at Raraba," "Bloodsong," "Incident at Mhlaba Jail," and "Death of the Nation" in *The Atlantic;* "An Interview" in *Grand Street;* "Tom and Beauty" in *Saturday Night;* and "Spirits Do Not Forgive" in *Radio Guide.*

To Isabel

Contents

Bloodsong

A Farm
at Raraba

MY LATE DAD was a magnificent shot. One time when
we were hunting in the Low Veld and had paused for a
smoke, there was the yelp of a wild dog, and a troop of
impala came bounding over the tall grass. Opposite us,
three hundred yards off, was a stony ridge like a wall,
six feet high. You would think those buck would avoid
it, but no, they went straight at it. One after the other,
without pausing or swerving, they leapt over it. They
cleared it by three or four feet. I tell you, friend, it was
a beautiful sight. You can't beat Nature for beauty, eh.

By the time the first two impala were over the ridge,
late Dad was ready, and as the next one leapt, Dad got
him. In midair. Same with the next one, and the next,
and the next. And the next. And the next. That was six
buck, one after the other.

Do you know, the wild dogs chasing those buck didn't
pause for the impala that late Dad had killed. They didn't
even react to the shots. They just followed one particular

buck that they had marked, and we saw them pull it down a couple of minutes later. You've got to hand it to Nature; she knows what she's doing.

But the most wonderful thing was when we got to the dead impala. Four of them were piled one on top of the other, neatly, like sacks in a store. Late Dad had shot each of them through the heart, at exactly the same point in its leap. The other two had been a bit slow. Late Dad had got each of them in the shoulder. If you can't get a head or a heart shot, the next best is the shoulder, because there's a lot of bone there, and if you hit bone it brings a creature down. It can't run, you see. The worst place is behind the heart, because then your bullet goes through a lot of soft entrails, eh. A gut-shot animal will sometimes run a couple of miles before it drops and you may never find it. When I hear of fellows shooting like that, it makes me want to put a slug into their guts and see how they would like to die that way.

Those impala were a bit of a problem. We only had a license for two and we only had the two mules we were riding. But God sent the ravens to Elijah, eh, so he sent us this Hottentot, Khamatjie. He worked crops on a share on the same farm as late Dad, but he was luckier with his farming — they live on the smell of an oil rag, those bastards. I don't mean "bastard" in a nasty way. I just mean there was a white father or grandfather, you understand. Well, thank God, this Khamatjie pitches up with his Ford pickup and a mincing machine, because he thought he would shoot a zebra. Nobody wants to eat zebra, but when it's sausage it's lovely; you call it beef or koodoo or eland. Late Dad and Khamatjie and I made impala sausages for two days.

In front of other white people Dad always treated Khamatjie like dirt, but otherwise he was very respectful,
because he was always borrowing money from Khamatjie
and getting drunk with him. He said Khamatjie didn't
mind supplying the brandy so long as he could say he
drank with a white man.

The training late Dad gave me in bushcraft and using
a rifle came in pretty handy when I was on the border of
South-West, doing my army service. The call-up inter-
rupts a man's career, if he's got a career, but a fellow that
hasn't had army has missed an experience — the outdoor
life, learning about musketry and map reading and section
leading, and who's what in these little frontline states,
and the tribes and the various movements in Angola and
Caprivi and Botswana. The big thing, though, is the
companionship. Until you've marched with four hundred
other chaps, all in step, all singing "Sarie Marais" or "Lili
Marlene" or "You can do with your loo loo what you
will" — until you've sat with five or six buddies in an
ambush, not daring to take a breath in case a guerrilla
gets you — until you've done things like that, you don't
know what loving your land and your folk is.

Out there, in the bundu, the action is sort of clean, like
they say it was in North Africa when we were fighting
Rommel in late Dad's war. Not like shooting little black
schoolgirls in the bum from inside an armored car. How
brave does a fellow have to be for that? I wonder what
these township heroes would do if they were faced with
Swapo guerrillas like my lot were.

Because I was keen and liked the bush, eh, I got to be
a sergeant, and they gave me six munts they had scratched
up in Damaraland, and sent us off across the border into

Angola. An intelligence probe, they said. Just these six munts, and me, and an intelligence corporal named Johan. He had had a course of interrogation training and his main job was to train these munts to get information out of prisoners. Scary stuff, man. You've got to hate a person to do it properly, or just hate people, eh.

Our first ten days on patrol yielded nothing. Then on the eleventh day, I had left Johan and the munts to fix our bivvie for the night while I went ahead for a looksee, at a big granite outcrop about two miles ahead. Just before I got to it there were shots from our camp, then some answering shots, then silence. I hid and waited quietly. After five minutes I saw four Swapies, running for all they were worth, along the side of a kopje half a mile away. They disappeared behind a dune, then bunched up on the big granite outcrop before the first Swapie launched himself off it to cross a crevasse. By that time I was ready, and I got him as he jumped. The next one was too close behind to stop, and I dropped him and number three as fast as it takes to press the trigger. The last one in the bunch pulled back, but I was quick and ready. I hit him, too. I heard the bullet ricochet off the rock, so I reckoned he was probably only wounded.

I was sure the first three would be dead, and I thought, Late Dad, look at that! Three in midair! And they're not impala, Dad. They're Royal Game.

Do you know about Royal Game? Late Dad told me, in the old days, before we became the Republic, anything that you were not allowed to shoot, because it was rare or useful, like tickbirds or ibises or oribi, was called Royal Game. Kids in those days believed it was because these birds or animals were reserved for the Royal Family to shoot. Fancy Prince Charles potting away at a flock of egrets or an iguana, eh! So Dad and his friends called desert natives Royal Game, because they are wild but you're not allowed to shoot them, see?

Like I told you, man, I can't bear to think of a gut-shot animal, lying in pain for hours. I felt the same way about this guerrilla, but I was on edge too. They say a wounded lion or buffalo is the most dangerous game in the wild, because he stalks the hunter. A wounded munt guerrilla must be worse, because he's got more IQ, eh, so I circled very cautiously round the granite rock. When I got opposite the crevasse I could see three bodies, one on top of the other, quite still. At eight hundred yards, three in three shots, it's a satisfaction, man.

And there, thank God, was guerrilla number four, just round the corner. He was standing upright in a narrow cleft in the rock, with one foot apparently stuck, and he was gripping his left bicep. A pressure point, I supposed. Through my field glasses I could see his left sleeve was a thick mat of blood. So all I had got was his arm. I found myself making excuses, thinking I had been slow because I used a peepsight. Late Dad always shot over open sights; he reckoned a sniper's eye aimed his hand, like a cowboy with a pistol, or a kid with a catapult.

The guerrilla's rifle was wedged above his head. For safety's sake I put a bullet into it. That left him unlikely to do much damage. When I edged my way closer I saw his leg was held fast in a crack, so he really was stuck and helpless. He was one of those yellow Hottentot types, with spaces between his peppercorns of hair, about my

age but as wrinkled as a prune. These Kalahari natives
go like that by the time they're twenty: it's the sun or
glands, I don't know. He was wearing a cast-off Cuban
tunic.

I climbed up the rock and looked down on him, trying
to remember the few words of local lingo I had picked
up from my men, but when he heard me he said in Afrikaans, "Good day, my baas."

I was pleased, I can tell you. It meant I could interrogate
him myself and, as he was our first prisoner, it would
show Johan and my black soldiers that I was one step
ahead of them, and it wasn't for nothing I was a sergeant.

The guerrilla bowed his head and pointed with his good
hand. "If you are going to shoot, make it two shots,
please, so that I will be properly dead."

"I don't shoot tethered goats," I said.

After a moment or two he looked up. "Can the goat
have some water?"

"First, talk."

"Yes, I talk, baas. What would baas like to talk about?"

I interrogated him, in the way we had been instructed,
using trick questions and repetitions. In case he was lying
or hiding anything I prodded his wounded arm once or
twice. He bore it as if he had it coming to him, but he
didn't appear to keep information back, and when his
voice cracked I passed down my water bottle.

His name was Adoons, which is a jokey way of saying
Adonis. It is what one calls a pet baboon. The farmer his
family had worked for called him that. Eventually his
own family stopped using the native name his father gave
him and almost forgot it. It seemed to belong to someone
else, Adoons said.

He had been a hunters' guide and a shepherd. When his family was pushed off the farm — for sheep stealing, it seemed — he joined the guerrillas who were fighting for Namibian independence. He had only the vaguest idea what the fighting was about. He knew it was against whites, but he had never heard of Namibia. Not surprising, when you think that there is no such place. He called it "South-West," just like we do. He moved from one guerrilla band to another, depending on how he liked the band's leader, and how much food or loot was available. His present band was under an Ndebele refugee from Zimbabwe. They were supposed to report to a General Kareo, but they had never seen him. I carefully recorded it all in my field notebook.

When I had done with questions, I sat back and lighted a cigarette. At the sound of the match he looked up. Smoking alone or drinking alone is not something a decent man wants to do; it's like making love alone, late Dad used to say. I gave Adoons the cigarette and lighted another one for myself.

He exhaled till his chest was flat, and then inhaled the smoke to fill his lungs. He held it for a long time before letting it out and saying, "Thank you, baas. Baas is a good man."

He smoked in deep gulps, keeping his head down. When he finished the cigarette he looked up. "Why didn't baas shoot when I was full of smoke?"

"I told you I don't shoot jackal bait," I said.

"I can see baas is a good man, but if baas's men find me here, they will do bad things to me. Perhaps it will take three days."

"I will tell them you have already talked."

"They will not care. They will torture me to make a game. My people will do it, too, if they catch one of your black soldiers. This is not Sunday school, my baas."

"We don't torture prisoners," I replied angrily. I knew he would not believe me.

"What will baas do with me?"

The fact was I didn't know what the hell I could do with Adoons. Once he has been interrogated, a native prisoner is worthless — worse, he would be a danger. He would have to be fed and guarded, and if he escaped he could give the enemy all sorts of valuable information. We didn't keep prisoners, except white men and Cubans: you could exchange or use them for propaganda.

As if sharing my problem, he said, "Has baas perhaps room for another shepherd on baas's farm?"

"I haven't got a farm and if I wanted a shepherd I would not employ a bloody Hottentot rebel."

"It is near sunset. Baas will go soon, before it gets dark. And when baas goes the hyenas will come. A hyena can bite right through a man's leg. A living man's leg."

I looked down at his skinny leg disappearing into the rock cleft, then climbed down and looked at his imprisoned foot. All I had to do was untie the laces and manipulate his ankle to get his foot out, leaving the boot behind. Then I gave the empty boot a kick and it came loose, too. Adoons wriggled till he found a purchase for his toes and raised himself a few inches.

"Give me your hand, Hottentot," I said. "I'll pull you out."

He put up his hand. I took him by the wrist and he clasped my wrist. With unexpected agility he braced his feet against the side of the cleft and scrambled up. I threw him his boot. When he stood up to catch it, his tunic opened to reveal a pistol loose in a leather holster on a broad, stylish belt round his waist.

He smiled shamefacedly. "I took it from the policeman who arrest me for stealing sheep."

"Is it loaded?"

"Oh, yes. Five bullets. I used one to learn to shoot it, but I've never fired it since. One has to be close to a man."

"You could have shot me."

"Yes, my baas. The pistol was stuck fast, like me, but when you were asking all those questions and leaning down to hear what I was saying, the barrel was pointing straight at you."

"Why didn't you shoot?"

"If baas was dead I would still be stuck in that rock with no one to help me before the soldiers or the hyenas came."

His wounded arm had been banged as he made his way up. It now began to bleed through the clot, not actively but *clthip, clthip, clthip*. Since I carried three field dressings, I could spare one. I dusted the antiseptic powder that came with it on Adoons's wound, bandaged it, and gave him one of the painkiller pills we were issued with.

"I would be a good shepherd for you. It is easy to work well for a kind master. Anyone can see baas will give good food, and a hut with a proper roof, and no sjambok whippings. Except for cheeky young men who have been to school."

"Come on, we must find a shelter for the night," I

said. I didn't like the thought of the hyenas he had talked about.

"These pills are good. The pain is quiet. Baas is like a doctor, eh? A sheep farmer has to be a doctor. I am very good with karakul ewes at lambing time. Baas knows, for the best fur you must kill the lambs as soon as they are born. Stillborn lambs are better. Their skins shine like black nylon with water spilled on it. It's messy, clubbing and skinning the little things without damaging the pelts. It's sad to hear all those ewes baa-ing. The meat is only fit for crows and vultures. But the rich ladies want the pelts before they get woolly."

He pointed out an overhanging rock twenty yards away. "Shall we spend the night there? Out of the dew, and it's open only on one side."

As we moved, I picked up dry sticks for kindling, but he put his hand on my arm. "If the soldiers see me in the firelight, or my people see baas, they will shoot."

I felt foolish and amateur.

"The dead men have clothes. Shall I fetch some?"

"We'll go together," I said. I wasn't going to get myself ambushed.

We went round the rock to the little cliff where the bodies lay. He whistled in admiration. "Baas shoots like a machine. These dead Ovambos look as if they've been arranged with a forklift truck." He added proudly, "I can drive a forklift. I learned on the sheep ranch."

We collected a couple of goatskins, a bush shirt with only a small blood patch, a water bottle, and a haversack of boiled ears of corn. There were three rifles. I grabbed two and took the bolts out of them. Adoons had already taken possession of the third. He grinned mischievously as he worked the bolt and demonstrated how he could use the rifle by tucking its butt under his sound arm.

"Now we can help each other, eh, baas. Like that bird that sits in a crocodile's mouth and cleans bits of meat out from between the crocodile's teeth. The crocodile does not eat him."

We settled down close together under the overhang and had an ear of corn each, and a pull from my hip flask. My dear old ma gave it to me when I was leaving for the border. "When you put it to your lips, it is your old momma kissing you," she said. I wondered what she would say if she knew she was kissing a Swapie Hotten-tot, too.

"Angora goats pay better than karakul sheep in the Dry Veld," Adoons said. "When I am the head shepherd, baas will give me a few sheep of my own. I will have a woman with buttocks that stick out so much you can use them for a stepladder. Ai! What fat yellow legs that woman has!" He sucked his breath in lasciviously. "Baas will have white girls in town but on the farm now and then a bushman girl. Ai, what a surprise he gets when he finds that the girl has an apron!" He described in detail the strip of skin some bushman women have hanging down from their gashes, and how some bushmen have an erection all the time, just like in the rock paintings.

I got sleepy and he shook me. "No sleep tonight," he said. "Listen." There were sounds of animals round the bodies. "Better we talk. Also it is good for a man and his mate to chat, isn't it?"

"I thought you fellows didn't want white men to have

farms," I said. "You want all the land for yourselves."

"Oh, yes. Yes, that's right. General Kareo says I will have a farm of my own. And a hundred sheep."

"Why stop at a hundred? Why not a thousand? Be a big boss. Make people call you *'Mr.* Adoons.'"

"How will I look after a thousand animals? I can't even count past twenty sheep without taking stones out of one pocket and putting them in the other. No, not a thousand. Unless — unless baas was my foreman." He laughed like a drunkard. "If my people win the war, will baas be my foreman? Please. Baas could have the big farmhouse and a motor car. Baas need not call me 'baas,' just 'Mr. Adoons.' Everything my foreman wants to do, he can do. Will my foreman be angry if some of the shepherds hide away when the police visit?"

"If your lot were the government, they would be your policemen."

"Policemen are policemen. Dogs' turds. Always after passes."

"Your lot say there won't be passes anymore."

"No passes! If people don't have passes, how can you trace a stock thief? What will we do if bad Ovambo kaffirs steal my karakuls?"

"That's your problem. Perhaps you'll have to get fierce German guard dogs."

"Oh, yes. That's a clever idea. My foreman will always find a way. Now, let's talk of nice things, not problems. What is baas's name?"

"Martinus."

"That is a friendly name for a foreman. In the evenings, after the shepherds have done their work and the sheep

and goats are in their thorn kraals, Mr. Adoons and Foreman Martinus will sit together and talk and look at the
veld. Ai, it's pretty country, between Platberg and the
Boa River. Short sweet grass and big flat-crown thorn
trees for shade. Animals eat the pods in the winter. There
are eland and koodoo and impala and bushpigs, but enough
grass for karakul sheep too."

"Sounds all right," I said.

"In the kloof there are wild bees and baboons. Ai, those
baboons! When a baboon finds a marula tree where the
plums have fermented, he gets as drunk as a man. Ai,
those drunk baboons! The leopards eat only baboons,
never sheep."

"Any water?"

"Water! There is the Boa River and big freshwater pans
full of barbel and eels and ducks, and widow birds with
long black tails like church deacons, and spur-wing geese
on the mud flats. The place is called Raraba. We shall sit
and drink buchu brandy and talk. Or just sit silent, like
old friends do."

"What the hell would you and I find to talk about?"

"Ai, pals' talk. About the grazing and the government
and women and hunting and what happens after you die.
I suppose baas knows lots of Jesus stories."

"I don't like buchu," I said.

"Do you like the kind of brandy called Commando?
They say it is good."

"Klipdrif is the best kind."

"Then we will have Klipdrif, Martinus."

"If it's hot and dry, one could irrigate a few acres for
a vineyard," I said.

"Does Martinus know about wine?"

"My grandfather used to make wine with grapes from his backyard."

"Ai, but this is lucky! So Foreman Martinus would grow grapes and make sweet wine. They say if you give a girl a bottle of that red Cape wine, her legs open before the bottle is finished. But I like brandy better."

"Me too," I said.

"Sometimes we will give a bottle of wine to the old people, too. On Mr. Adoons's farm the laborers can stay even when they are too old to work. And when the rations are given out, the old people get meat and mealie-meal, too, just like the others. Is that right, Martinus?"

"If the baas says so," I said.

At first light we stretched and scouted. There was no activity. Adoons tore a sleeve out of a dead guerrilla's shirt; I made a sling and tied his wounded arm against his chest. He kept a grip on the rifle all the time.

I offered him my flask, and we each took a swallow. He handed me one of the two ears of corn left in the haversack, and pointed south. "Foreman Martinus must walk that way. I will go north."

"Good luck, Mr. Adoons. I'll come and visit you at your farm at Raraba after the war, and see if you still need a foreman."

"Ai, Martinus," he said, "we will drink and talk, eh. Ai, how we will talk!" He knocked his rifle barrel against mine, like clinking a glass, and set off.

I slid behind the rock where I could watch him without exposing myself. Late Dad used to say if you trust a

Hottentot you might as well wear a cobra for a necklace;
so I kept my crossed hairs on him, expecting him to whirl
round any moment and loose off, or to disappear behind
a boulder or thick shrub and perhaps circle round to take
me in the rear. However, he walked very deliberately up
the hill, and did not dodge behind trees or rocks like an
experienced veld man would, nor did he look back to see
what I was doing.

When he reached the top of the kopje he stood for some
moments silhouetted against the sky and waved his gun.
Challenging me to shoot? When he disappeared over the
top, I quickly shifted to another position a couple of
hundred yards away so that if he crawled round to the
side of the kopje I would be ready for him. By sunup
nothing had happened, so I decided he was on his way
to find his band. He would probably keep the field dress-
ing I put on his arm and pretend that he had shot a South
African soldier.

I found my chaps easily enough — I told them I could
have shot three or four of them if I had been a guerrilla —
and sent them to see what they could find on the Swapies
I had shot; even those fellows sometimes have letters or
helpful papers.

You would think a man's second-in-command would
want to say a warm word about the marksmanship. The
blackies were impressed, but Johan said, "You shouldn't
have shot to kill, Sarge. We're not in the humane hunting
business, you know. A dead Swapie is nafi, isn't he?" He
liked showing off his intelligence jargon, like using "nafi"
to mean "not available for interrogation."

I shut up about Adoons. My blackies might have been

able to pick up his trail and perhaps find him before he rejoined his lot, especially if his wound started bleeding again. Then, if they roughed him up a bit, he could hardly avoid giving the whole story away, and that would mean a court-martial for me, wouldn't it?

We eventually caught a few Swapies. I did not like Johan's attitude, but he was right — a dead prisoner is nafi — so I shot for the leg and told the men to do the same. I stood by with a submachine gun at the ready during the interrogations in case any of the prisoners knew about me and Adoons. Fortunately, none did.

When I finished my army I took my discharge there in South-West and went to have a look at the Platberg area and especially Raraba.

It is nice country, if you like desert, and a man could pick up a thousand hectares cheap from fellows who are getting cold feet about the UN. Also the market for Persian lamb — that's karakul — is looking up again, now that Greenpeace has stopped women from buying baby seal. Some sheep ranchers say they would send Greenpeace a donation if it wasn't for the currency restrictions.

I followed the Boa River up to Platberg. The river runs against the mountain cliffs, so there is no space in between for a farm. I thought I must have misunderstood Adoons.

That evening there was a drunk lying asleep in the gutter outside the hotel. The doorman laughed when I bent down to shake the man.

"Leave him, mister," he said. "He's happier in Raraba."

It turns out that is what the Hottentots around there call a lullaby, a dreamland that is too nice to be real. At first I was disappointed. Then I thought, Just as well. Suppose a man had a nice sheep ranch, and then one day a bloody old yellow Hottentot pitched up and said, "Martinus, old friend, do you remember your baas, Mr. Adoons? I've brought a bottle of Klipdrif brandy. That's the kind you like, isn't it? Let us sit and drink and talk pals' talk."

It would be embarrassing, eh.

The Self-Destruction
of the Ama Gabe

AN ETHNO-DEMOGRAPHIC NOTE

IN PRECOLONIAL AFRICA the poet was recognized both as
the transmitter of society's history and as the extoller of
its living heroes, and was honored accordingly. Chaka's
laureate, Magolwane, is a well-known example.

In some clans the office was hereditary, the heir ap-
parent being trained from childhood to recite histories
and to compose songs celebrating current events. At least
one such position appears to have survived. The incum-
bent is an aged woman, one Lucy Mahlekane, who claims
to be the last in a line of female poet-historians unique
to the Ama Gabe clan. She is, as far as the writer knows,
the only instance so far noted of a Bantu Sappho.

The author made her acquaintance during the course
of his excavation of the smelting site known as Dabula's
Pit. (A description of the dig will shortly appear in *The
Journal of African Archaeology*.) She was a constant and

curious observer of the archaeological operations. The author's explanations of his activities, coupled with some small financial tokens of appreciation, induced her to relate the traditional story of the events leading to the abandonment of this ancient ironworks.

Her account constitutes the main body of this paper. Some introductory remarks may, however, be helpful.

First, as regards the Ama Gabe themselves: now hardly distinguishable as an entity, the remnants of the clan are to be found between the Nkwala and Mgabe rivers. Modern Gabe are Zulu-speaking but some of Lucy's more archaic constructions suggest a Tonga connection.

Second, self-genocide, or something close to it, is not without precedent in southern Africa; witness the voluntary restriction of birth rate by the Herero in response to German colonial repression; and the Ama Xhosa cattle killing of 1857. (Soga, *The Southeastern Bantu,* relates how Xhosa tribesmen were persuaded by a prophetess, Nongqause, to destroy their grain and cattle on the promise of greater herds and full granaries, to be supplied by the spirits, who would then help to drive out both the white invaders of Xhosa territory and also those Xhosas who had adopted European-style trousers in lieu of skin kilts. Some twenty-five thousand persons and 200,000 cattle are estimated to have perished. Xhosa military power, until then a formidable brake on British expansion, was broken forever.)

The following narrative is a translation of Mrs. Lucy Mahlekane's own words, transcribed from the author's tape recordings made over a two-week period. They have been edited only insofar as has been necessary to eliminate repetitions, extraneous conversations, and obscurities that were clarified in later discussions.

Lucy says:

"When mankind first came out from the reeds, each person had a skill. One could hunt, another could tan skins, a third could cook corn, a fourth brew beer, and so on. Many of the people then found it convenient to share skills. The woman who could cook corn taught other women how to do it, and the women who could brew beer or grow pumpkins taught the cook how to do these things. That is what most people did. But Galo, who had been given the secret of persuading stones to give birth to iron, and Galombili, who was given the knowledge of producing copper, would not trade their secrets with other men. Galombili tried to steal the secret of iron from Galo, but Galo caught him and they fought. Iron is harder than copper, so Galo won easily. Galombili died before Galo could squeeze his secret from him. That is why our people never could make copper.

"Galo said, 'I will not share my secret. I will make axes, spears, and hoes, and sell them for cows and corn and wives.'

"He taught all his sons to work iron, but taught only one son to smelt ore. His people did as he did and traded iron things for sheep and goats, pots, baskets, and beads. They became very rich and much feared. Because they had so much iron they could afford long stabbing spears, not merely little iron tips on their spears, such as other tribes had. Some nations count wealth in wives or cattle, but in those days a Gabe man weighed his pride by the number of weapons of war that he possessed.

"He gave each spear a name, like a person, and sang

to it: 'Sharp thing, sharp thing that kills men, shine bright for your master.'

"The time when iron was most needed was when a new regiment was enrolled. Every few years the generals would summon all the youths who had been initiated and newly circumcised, and turn them into soldiers. Each new soldier received a stabbing spear, a throwing spear, and a shield. As soon as the youngest regiment was ready, the men in the oldest regiment could go home and take wives.

"Now, when the Nkonka regiment, the Bushbuck Rams, was created, there were more youths than the generals and the spear makers had expected, and so there were not enough spears ready. The generals knew that Pila, the chief, would be very angry. They remembered that years ago, when the generals had not arranged for enough oxhide shields, Pila had handed the generals over to the young soldiers, saying, 'Flay them and use their skins to make shields.'

"In fear they ran quickly to Dabula, the smelter. He was a descendant of Galo, and was the only sorcerer who could make stones give birth to metal. The generals gathered scores of girls, and some warriors, and sent them to fetch iron stones. They gave the girls baskets of corn to carry on their heads. 'It will take four days to the place of iron stones and six days back,' they said to the girls. 'Cache two basketsful of corn out of three on your journey out so that you will have enough food when you are carrying heavy loads on your way back. And at night, sleep three girls to a mat so that you will not be able to seduce any young warriors.'

"To the warriors they said, 'Guard the girls from enemies but do not burden yourselves by carrying stones. You may need your strength. Above all, keep chaste, for intercourse will pollute the iron and weaken it. No one who works with iron can have intercourse, for iron must be pure. When you return, you may indulge again. Now, go as fast as you can.'

"Meantime the charcoal burners burned gqeba trees, and the wives and daughters of the smelters gathered and softened clay; then they wove big rush baskets and coiled thick ropes of clay round them and plastered the clay down hard to make smelting ovens. They did not smooth over the outside of the oven pots. Each girl liked to leave the imprint of her hand in the clay.

"While others did these tasks, some of Dabula's men had gone on an evil hunt. It is a dreadful thing, but how can sorcery be done only with nice things? They went out to kill a man and take parts of his body, for no metal will be born if the stones are not fed with the fat of a human being. Where do you Europeans get the fat to make all those railway tracks and other iron things? I am sure that the fat does not come from white people.

"The girls who had gone to fetch ore returned, the charcoal burners brought their coals, and the potters finished the ovens, but the man hunters came back empty-handed. You see, the first man they aimed for saw them and cried out before they killed him, so he was not suitable for medicine. The flesh of a victim who sees his killers has no potency. Then they stalked a girl, but she had a lover, so he and she were looking both ways, as embracing lovers do. It was the same with every other victim they stalked.

"The generals threatened Dabula. He and his men were now ready to take anyone, even someone from their own neighborhood. Of course, everybody in the neighborhood quickly knew. In each kraal sentries were appointed and fires were kept burning all night. When people walked abroad they went in groups, with one or two walking backwards, or carried children on their shoulders, facing to the rear. Children play such a game even today. It is called 'Outwitting Dabula's Men.'

"The man hunters failed, of course, and soon Dabula was desperate. In the dead of night he went silently into the hut of his wife, Tala, and took their sleeping baby. He put one hand over the child's eyes so that it could not see him, and the other hand over its mouth, and took it to the smelting pit. He wept, even though he was a grown man, and sang, 'Let my tears mix with the body that is Little Dabula. He would have carried the secrets of our ancestors.' Then he strangled the little boy and took the fat he needed for his iron making.

"When Tala awoke and found her child missing and smelled the smoke from the smelting pit, she knew the truth. She waited and wept and pretended to search. She screamed that a leopard or a wild dog must have taken the baby. Some brave men helped her search. They killed a leopard, and she made as if she believed it was the animal that had eaten her child.

"At the same time she started brewing very strong beer. She went to a witch doctor for aphrodisiac herbs. On the eighth day, when the beer was ready, she skimmed the froth and added the herbs, and bathed, and rubbed herself with umtomboti perfume. She gave Dabula the beer and asked him to comfort her, and she rubbed herself against him and fondled him, as women know how, until he no longer resisted. He had intercourse with her though he knew it was forbidden. Then she laughed and sang, 'A thing that is soft after love. A blade no enemy need fear.'

"The smelters made iron and gave it to the smiths. The smiths forged blades and gave them to the spearwrights, and the spearwrights bound the blades into shafts with strong glue and lengths of fresh hide from a cow's tail. Do you know wet cowhide shrinks hard like iron when it is dry?

"The generals gave the spears to the young men, the witch doctors sprinkled medicines on them, and the chief named the regiment Nkonka, the Bushbuck Rams. A bushbuck ram has sharp horns and fears no one. He does not hide, but barks aloud in the night.

"Then the chief sent the Bushbuck Rams on an expedition. He chose an easy mission to heat their blood and make them feel good. They were to punish a little clan that had refused to pay the tribute it owed. The brave young men, the Bushbucks, attacked the enemy fiercely, and stabbed and stabbed. But when the enemy held up their shields, the spear blades of the Bushbucks bent at the tips. The iron was soft like that thing that Dabula's wife, Tala, sang about. The hearts of the enemy grew strong, and they turned on the Bushbucks, even though the Bushbucks were Gabe.

"Some of the young men died; others fled. When the survivors reassembled, they marched on Dabula's place and killed him with their bent-tipped spears. They killed him and all his helpers and servants, and then all the smiths who forged weapons. They killed every single man who knew how to make stones beget iron, or how to work iron.

"When Pila, the chief, heard of it he cried, 'The strength is gone from the Ama Gabe! Galo has left us. Woe, woe to the Bushbucks.' He summoned all the other regiments of his army, even the men who had been allowed to marry. Then he waited for the Bushbucks to report. When they arrived and laid down their shields to go into the chief's enclosure, the chief cried, 'Hla!' Then the other regiments fell on them and slaughtered them. They killed their own young brothers with whom they had laughed and played, because the chief commanded it. They sang, 'Little brother, whom I loved, I stab you deep, once only, to spare your pain.' Then there were no men of that age group left in the tribe, only mature men, and boys who were not yet of age for initiation.

"Now there was no new iron. If a man lost an axe or a woman a hoe, there was no replacement. The Ama Gabe needed many things that other tribes made, because they had been used to buying them from the other tribes and had not learned to make them for themselves. They bartered the iron they still had, but soon they did not have enough. Other clans discovered that the Ama Gabe were short of weapons and sneered at them.

"At first the Ama Gabe women tried to grow corn by poking the ground with digging sticks and ox horns, but they soon got tired and told their fathers and husbands, 'Give us your spears for hoes or else there will be no corn or pumpkins or grain for beer.'

"The men relinquished their weapons and helped the women heat them and hammer them flat into hoes. They made pointed sticks for themselves and tipped them with bone for hunting. But being without iron weapons, the symbols of manhood, the men felt like eunuchs. They were so ashamed, they did not attend the tribal council. Their women went instead, and a woman became the chief's adviser. Also, the men were too ashamed to relate the tale, and so a woman, that same Tala, wife of Dabula, became the reciter of tales and songs for the clan. When she died, her daughter was the singer, then her daughter, down to me. But I have only sons. So it is good that you take down my words.

"Soon afterwards white traders came, bringing iron implements, which they exchanged for ivory. The Ama Gabe men were able to throw away their bone weapons, and they recovered some of their self-esteem. Also, because there were very few young men, many girls remained unmarried long after puberty, even though their fathers were prepared to accept low bride-prices. The girls vied with each other for men's favors, and the men again took to giving women orders, but they were never again as arrogant and lazy as before."

That, then, is the legend. As might be expected, Lucy has no way of dating the events she relates, other than that they occurred "in the time of my great-grandmother Tala." She gives her genealogy as follows: Lucy, daughter of Beauty, daughter of Antonia, daughter of Noxale, daughter of Sika, daughter of Mako, daughter of Nomanga, daughter of Tala the wife of Dabula son of Keli, son of Mahanda. (Note the reversion to patrilineality when we reach Dabula.) Accepting Lucy's own estimate of her age as sixty, and allowing an average of twenty years per generation, we arrive at a time frame some two hundred years ago; that is, circa 1785. This brings us within a decade of what appears to be the only previous written reference to the decline and fall of the Ama Gabe, namely, Major John Barnet Foxton's *Report Concerning the Late Disaffection Amongst Kaffirs North of the Inqualah River*, 1775. Foxton attributes the breakdown of order largely to a shortage of iron.

> Cessation of the smelting activities, formerly practised by the smiths of Gabeland, induced a metal famine and a consequent beating of swords, not indeed into scriptural ploughshares, but certainly into hoes. Whether this followed upon, or was induced by, the emergence of female tribal councillors was not established. Certain it is that Gabe women now enjoy authorities and prerogatives previously confined to their fathers and brothers.

Lucy passes no judgment on the events she relates, except that it is sad that the clan lost its wealth and power. Major Foxton is more expansive. He comments:

> Deprived of their ancient occupation, namely, war, or rather the accumulation of arms in readiness for war, these once-disciplined and peremptory soldier-traders sank within a generation to be docile peasants, more deferential to their wives than to their captains, and attentive less to arms than to flocks and festivals. What lesson this may hold for Christian nations can only be a matter for melancholy conjecture.

An Interview

THE SPECIAL BRANCH OFFICIAL stopped at her gate, looked for a longish time at the nameplate M. P. HOFMEYR, as if it had importance, then came up the steps and knocked. He was a neat, ordinary-looking, freckled man, wearing a Hertzog High School Old Boys' blazer.

He introduced himself as Mr. Peter Gunter, showed his plastic identification card, and suggested that Mrs. Hofmeyr might want to telephone the local police station to check. He waited until she asked him in, and stood until she invited him to sit down.

"Well, Mr. Gunter, what can I do for you?" She spoke tartly, to keep the apprehension out of her voice. She thought of herself as nonpolitical, by which she meant that she did not belong to a political party; but she had stood in line with other black-sashed women in the days when such gestures seemed significant, and she was one of the few people to whom Emma Dupreez said goodbye before she fled across the border to Lesotho.

AN INTERVIEW

Mr. Gunter took a notebook from his side pocket. It was thin and flat so that it would not spoil the smooth fit of his blue melton blazer. He did not open the notebook but looked briefly at it, as though refreshing his mind on some detail that he could read through the black cover.

It was characteristic of Emma Dupreez that even when she was in flight from the security police her laughter was as frequent and uninhibited as ever. She had described hilariously how Rhoda Cohen had dressed in her, Emma's, clothes. Emma demonstrated how Rhoda had had to pad her hips and bosom and to practice Emma's flaunting walk. Rhoda left through the front door; within thirty seconds they saw the surveillance man move off from the next corner to follow her. A few minutes later Emma slipped through the servant's quarters to the old sanitary lane that ran behind the house — the "shit street," Emma called it, as they had done in their childhood, when it was the route for a cart that collected night soil from backyard outhouses. She strolled down the lane and dodged through an empty yard into the next lane, where she waited for Sammy Govinder to pick her up in his taxi — his conspicuous, broken-down Indian taxi, for God's sake! They were late and Sammy was anxious to leave, but Emma had insisted that she must first say goodbye to Mrs. Hofmeyr.

Mr. Gunter glanced from his notebook to the portrait of Mrs. Hofmeyr's husband. "I remember the late doctor came and made a speech at our prize giving once. They gave me a prize, too. For attendance." He smiled self-deprecatingly. "It was all they could find to praise me for." He had widely spaced teeth, like that comedian who used to say he parted his teeth in the middle. It is supposed to be a sign of good nature.

Mrs. Hofmeyr did not want to have a human being–to–human being conversation with Mr. Gunter, but habitual courtesy surfaced before she could control it. "Oh, I'm sure you undervalue yourself, Mr. Gunter," she said.

She had given Emma her gold bracelet. It was inscribed from her husband: *MPH from RH*. It was the only valuable piece of jewelry she still had. The rest was in a deposit box in a London bank; her niece in Scotland had the receipt and the key. Her husband had said, "Just in case. Just in case things blow up here. It will be a way of raising a little unauthorized foreign exchange in an emergency. Diamonds are a refugee's best friend."

Mr. Gunter said, "You are M. P. Hofmeyr, isn't it?"

"You know that, I suppose, Mr. Gunter. Or were you expecting to see someone else?"

He did not change expression. "Mrs. Hofmeyr, there are many facts known to the authorities that we nevertheless still always try to verify with the parties concerned. It is procedure, you understand. Procedure and evidence. Mistaken identity is always unfortunate. It is not nice for an innocent person to have her name on a dossier, like suppose a clerk gets the papers mixed up because he does not understand the information-retrieval system."

He mistook her frown for a question. "It is what we used to call Records and Filing," he explained.

"Please get to your point, Mr. Gunter." She spoke irritably, waiting for him to produce whatever frightening thing he had come to ask or say.

He looked at his notebook, flat in his left hand, opened it, then put it in his pocket. "You and your son, John Hofmeyr, have social relations with Bantu female Edith Xulu" — he struggled with the click and made the name come out as Kulu — "and her son Z. K. Matthews Xulu. Is that correct?"

Relief washed over her. It was only about the Xulus. Two years ago, during the riots, John ran into an African mob. He was knocked down and was being kicked by a lot of feet when someone intervened, standing straddling him. It was Z. K. Matthews Xulu. He came home with John as far as the gate. When they parted John said, "You saved my life. Some time I'll try to do the same for you." Z.K. smiled. "I will appreciate that, man."

She said, "Yes, we are friends of the Xulus." She was irritated to find herself pronouncing the name as badly as Mr. Gunter did. "And what's it got to do with you? It's not a crime to be friendly with a native, much as your precious minister might like to make out that it is."

"I wanted to ask for your help about Edith Xulu."

"My help?" She spoke shrilly now, with courage. "You mean you've come here trying to get something out of me to help you trap those simple, honest people. Well, you've come to the wrong place, Mr. Gunter. Put that in your dossier."

Mr. Gunter remained sitting. He took his notebook from his side pocket, turned a page, and closed it.

"Have you recently lost a gold bracelet?"

"No," she said, hoping her voice was steady.

"A fourteen-karat gold bracelet, inscribed *MPH from RH,* was recently found by the police." He spoke without inflection.

She was silent.

"Is it not your bracelet?"

"It was mine, but I gave it away."

"Could I ask to whom?"

She saw no point in prevarication. "To Emma Dupreez."

"How long have you known Bantu female Xulu?"

She had never had Africans, other than servants, in her house. When John invited Z. K. Matthews Xulu and his mother to dinner, she was so nervous she nearly fell ill, fearing heaven knows what breaches of taste or tact she, or the Xulus, would commit. Mrs. Xulu put her at ease in a matter of minutes, admiring her sewing and making little jokes. She was especially funny about Z.K.'s name. Her husband had much admired an African university lecturer of that name, but neither she nor her son had been able to discover what the initials stood for. When they were depressed they made up hilarious combinations of sounds to fit the letters.

"I've known Mrs. Xulu for about two years," Mrs. Hofmeyr said. "What has that got to do with anything?"

"Mrs. Hofmeyr, people from old important families don't always know what goes on in the communities." He saw her puzzled look. "The nonwhite communities," he explained. "You know, like I know, some people don't like white people to have black friends. Especially if their black friends visit them in their houses. They say it is bad for property values. Yes, we all know that is so, isn't it? But do we also realize that some blacks don't like blacks to have white friends?"

He paused to let the thought sink in. "When there is trouble, like a riot, or just a bit too much brandy or home brew, then there's usually one or two murders. Do you know, Mrs. Hofmeyr, there are more murders in this one little black township every year than there are white murders in the whole province? But I suppose a person must not be too severe about these things. All nations have their own forms of self-expression, isn't it?"

He waited for Mrs. Hofmeyr to acknowledge what he was saying, and leaned forward. "So now, say, there are a few drunks and they feel angry. There's a lot of anger inside these fellows, you know. What the professors like to call aggression. Sometimes it is not enough for them to stab one another. They look for another kind of target, a political target, perhaps. Like maybe we would if we were in their place."

Against her desire to keep Mr. Gunter at a distance, Mrs. Hofmeyr found herself nodding.

Mr. Gunter went on. "So when a few tsotsis are looking for a target, there is someone like your friend Edith Xulu, what they call an Uncle Tom, a Bantu that likes being friends with white people. She is one of those old-fashioned mission kaffirs, excuse me, Christian Africans. Completely detribalized. They've got no pride in their nation. They want to be like Europeans."

Mrs. Xulu was vehement and amusing about race relations. "Z.K. is mad. They are all mad, these young people who want black power. If you throw out the white people, the whole place will be like the homelands, I tell him. Look how it was before the white people came, I say. No Jesus, no motorcars, no soap, no nylon, no brandy, no wireless; just kaffir beer and assegais and ngoma dancing, and skins to wear. Do you know what they gave my grandmother when she was a bride? They gave her an isidwaba, a skin skirt, to last all her life. All her life, madam, and you can't wash it. That is what it will be like, I tell Z.K.''

Mrs. Hofmeyr waited for Mr. Gunter to conclude. He in turn looked at her as if expecting a response. When she remained silent he said, ''A person might think they were being kind when they were doing the opposite.''

Mrs. Hofmeyr still said nothing.

Mr. Gunter opened his notebook and looked hard at it. Mrs. Hofmeyr could see that the page was blank. He closed the book and said, ''We would appreciate your cooperation. Edith Xulu is important to us.''

''Important to you? What do you mean?''

How could Edith be important to them? Was he hinting that she was a police informer? No, surely not. She was a lovely, open person. And yet — she did seem to have much more money than one would expect. . . .

Mrs. Hofmeyr stared at Mr. Gunter with horror. He gave a tiny, knowing nod as if to confirm what she was thinking and somehow to suggest that he and Mrs. Hofmeyr were on the same wavelength about Mrs. Xulu. The implication infuriated Mrs. Hofmeyr, but before she could find the words to repudiate it, Mr. Gunter reached into an inner pocket and produced a bracelet. "Is that yours?"

Mrs. Hofmeyr took it and pretended to examine it. It was obviously her bracelet. Mr. Gunter said, "If a piece of found property is not claimed, it is *res derelictae,* nobody's property. It is eventually sold and the money goes into the Police Orphans' Fund. You may as well have it back. I don't think anyone else will claim it."

"Where did you get it?"

"It was thrown from a vehicle that was attempting to evade the police."

It was just like Emma: to bungle the arrangements for secretly crossing the border — the police could probably trace her halfway across town by her laugh and the smoke trail of Sammy Govinder's taxi — and yet to have the presence of mind to throw away the bracelet, hoping that she would thus avoid implicating Mrs. Hofmeyr. Poor dear, where have they got her now?

"Where is Mrs. Dupreez?" she asked. Her voice sounded strangled.

Instead of answering, Mr. Gunter reached again into his inner pocket and held out a half sheet of paper. It was a typed receipt. "If you'll just sign at the bottom," he said, producing a silver pen. The pen was thin and flat, designed to fit snugly in the wearer's pocket without making a bulge. She signed. Mr. Gunter smiled, showing spaced teeth and pink gums, and put the receipt and pen back into his inner breast pocket.

"Where is Mrs. Dupreez?" Mrs. Hofmeyr repeated.

He looked surprised, as if she had revived a subject

they had already disposed of. "Where do you expect her to be?"

Did that mean they didn't have her? Or that everyone should know where political detainees were kept? There was that place in Johannesburg. . . . And what about poor Sammy Govinder?

"Can I see her?"

"You will have to make your own arrangements for that, Mrs. Hofmeyr."

Did that mean they did have her?

"Do you happen to have your passport handy?"

"What do you want it for?"

"I think you will find it expires next May. May twentieth, isn't it?"

She went to her desk, took out her passport, and looked at the expiration date. It was May 20. Mr. Gunter half rose and held out his hand politely, as if to receive a cup of tea.

What would he do if she refused to give it to him? Probably insist on his right to inspect an item of government property: there was that statement about the passport's belonging to the government, not to you, wasn't there? Suppose he kept it? Please God, don't let him keep it.

She handed the passport to him. He did not open it but rested it on his knee.

"Did you give anything else to Mrs. Dupreez?"

She shook her head.

"Did she give you anything? Or leave anything with you to keep for her? Any papers?"

One of Emma's parting jokes was a request to the post

office to re-address her mail. She gave as her forwarding address the apartment of her cousin, who was now an attaché or secretary of some kind at the embassy in Washington. "I wonder how he'll explain that away," Emma had said exultantly. "He was such a righteous liberal when we were at college. And look at him now. Spineless little cryptonationalist arse creeper."

"She left a letter for me to post," Mrs. Hofmeyr said.

Mr. Gunter tensed. "Have you got it?"

"No, of course not. I posted it."

"Did you notice who it was for?"

"The postmaster."

Mr. Gunter frowned. "The postmaster? Here?"

"Yes."

He picked up her passport, looked at the photo and then at her, and flipped over two or three pages.

"Yes, it expires May twentieth." He weighed the document in his left hand. "You should not leave it too late. Sometimes applications for renewal take a very long time. Because of all the inquiries involved, you know. It's what people call red tape, but there is always a reason for a procedure, not so?"

He put the passport back on his knee. "Where was Mrs. Dupreez aiming for when you saw her?"

Mrs. Hofmeyr was silent. Mr. Gunter opened the passport again and carefully looked at the stamps on one page. He said "Hmmm" very quietly, took out his pen, and put it in to mark the place; he seemed to be comparing the stamps with those on another page, and looked inquiringly at her. He said nothing. He looked again at her passport, kept open at that place by his flat silver pen, and back at her.

"She was going to Lesotho."

Surely they must already know. That car evading the police must have been on the road to Lesotho. Emma had not said that the fact that Lesotho was her destination should be kept secret. Perhaps everyone would know that that was where she would head for in the first instance. Botswana would be a better place, because it was not surrounded by South African territory, but it was much farther. But perhaps Emma had assumed she, Mrs. Hofmeyr, would naturally keep it secret. If Emma had got through, perhaps it wouldn't matter whether the police knew. Or perhaps they knew anyway, through their informers: people said they had dozens of agents in all these little countries. If Mr. Gunter took the passport away, what could she do? You couldn't go to court about it. Suppose Emma hadn't got through? If the police had her in custody, they wouldn't be asking about her destination, would they? So she might be in hiding, waiting for another chance to cross the border, and now the police would know which roads to watch. Dear Lord, what had she done to Emma?

"Lesotho. Yes." Mr. Gunter gave a little pleased nod. "If you don't mind my saying so, that desk is not a very secure place for a valuable article like a passport. Why don't you keep it in your bank with your jewelry? I suppose a lady like you must have a lot of diamond rings and things like that."

He dropped his voice, as if giving away important

official information to a friend. "We notice ladies don't wear so many valuable items nowadays. Perhaps it's because they have illegally hidden them overseas, eh?"

He once again put his pen back in his breast pocket, and held out the passport to Mrs. Hofmeyr. She took it and held it tight with both her hands on her lap, resisting the temptation to press it to her heart.

Mr. Gunter leaned forward. "In regard to Bantu female Xulu . . ."

The Going Home
of Ntambo

I HAD A FRIEND who was a Zulu witch doctor. He had
many fearsome native names, like Eyes in the Dark Forest
and Witches Fear Him, but he usually told white people
his name was Charlie, because it sounded so mild and
innocent. He had a great reputation for knowing things
that had occurred in secret, and wrongdoers were careful
not to be present when he was divining, lest the bones
should smell them out. Charlie was also very good at
dealing with bad magic, and sometimes even foretold
misfortunes and illnesses that had not yet happened but
were going to be brought on by an enemy's evil mach-
inations. The most common symptoms were sleepless-
ness, stomach discomfort, and headaches, or, in the case
of young women, uncontrollable hysterical giggling or
cuckoo noises. He was rarely wrong in these predictions,
and never failed to cure the condition for a small fee, such
as a lamb or a few chickens. In grave cases an ox might
be required. White people also consulted him — openly

about lost articles and strayed animals, and surreptitiously about love affairs.

I had seen him occasionally at native ceremonies, but I did not get to know him until he called at the farm one day during my school holidays, having heard that I was also practicing magic. I was having fun at the time with *Teach Yourself Conjuring,* and with experiments on capturing methane from an oil drum filled with decaying cow dung; it can be lighted to create will-o'-the-wisps on dark nights.

Charlie arrived in full regalia — monkey-tail kilt, ankle- and kneebands of rattling insect cocoons, a necklace of small antelope horns full of fats and herbs, a headband of rats' skulls, and a large skin bag full of animal knuckle-bones and other divining materials, suspended from an old Sam Browne belt. Two slivers of white wood protruded from his mouth to simulate a pair of fangs.

He had also brought his female baboon. On all fours, she was as big as an Alsatian, and when she stood on her hind legs she reached to his shoulder. She sat next to him, lunging and snarling whenever a dog came near. If anyone spoke harshly to her, or showed his teeth, even in a smile, she took it as a threat and crouched, presenting her red rump in submission. When she did so the witch doctor laughed and taunted the embarrassed man: "Look, she loves you. Do you love her?"

It was said that she had a part-human child, a small black hairy person called a tikoloshi, who roamed about at night, doing mischief. It is very unlucky to meet a tikoloshi, which is one of the reasons why decent people do not walk alone in the dark.

The witch doctor sat waiting for me outside the kitchen door. When I appeared he saluted me, respectfully removed his fangs, sat down so as to put himself on a level below me, and inquired after my father. I was pretty sure he had chosen to come on a day when he knew my father would be away. I let him talk of the recent floods, the doings of the antimalaria campaign, and how fat our cattle were. He waited for me to ask him his business, but I did not, wanting to see how long it would be before he had to be discourteous and volunteer it.

We were still fencing with each other when the foreman struck the big plough disc to signal the midday meal. A number of laborers crowded round us, saying excitedly to the witch doctor, "Watch! Watch! He will whistle up fire!" Within a minute or so a wisp of smoke curled up from a little pile of paper on a flat stone near us; the paper burst into flame, igniting a pyramid of kindling stacked above it. I fed the blaze a few small sticks. The laborers shouted with glee, "Can you do that, reader of bones?"

The witch doctor watched carefully. "Is it permitted to look close?" He picked up a burning stick, smelled it, scratched at what was left of the kindling. Then he saw the magnifying glass in its wire frame. "Is this it?" he asked.

I had rigged it up so that the sun would shine through it at midday. It had to be adjusted every three or four days. I showed him how it operated, and he tried it on the back of his hand until it burned. "It is a clever trick," he said.

I held it out as if to give it to him. He put out his hand to take it. There was nothing there. (Sleight-of-Hand

Exercise 17 in the conjuring book.) He let his jaw drop and gazed reproachfully at my empty hand. "Ha! A great medicine!" he said as I took the lens out of my pocket to give him. He received it, then opened his hand. It was empty, but with his other hand he picked the lens, a small dead bird, and a number of beads out of the cuff of my trousers. I said, "Ha! A great medicine!" and beat the ground as boys do to admit defeat in a wrestling match.

He motioned to his bag of bones. "Will you hear what they say?"

If I agreed, every native in the district, and sooner or later every white person, would know and believe whatever rubbish or slander the witch doctor chose to invent about me. On the other hand, if I refused, the laborers would think I was scared, and besides, I would have missed something rather exciting.

I said carelessly, "It seems to be a day for games."

Before I had finished speaking, he made a quick movement, spreading twenty or thirty knucklebones in a white crescent on the ground between us. The natives shrank back to leave a safe distance between themselves and the bones. It took a good deal of self-control for me not to recoil too, but I stood my ground, even though a couple of bones rolled close to my feet.

Bleached animal skulls and ribs look sinister, but knucklebones do not. They do not even look like bones — more like dimpled cubes such as one might make by taking small blocks of white clay and lightly pressing one's fingers into each pair of opposite sides. Children use them for dice, or to represent herds of cattle or companies of warriors. The sheep and ox bones in front of

me were not different from those that children play with,
except that they seemed to shift and distort as I stared at
them. When I looked up they stayed steady for a moment,
but then they stirred again, as if they were alive, and
began to form patterns — a triangle or a spearhead, and
a crab with long curving claws that came and went.

The witch doctor poked a finger at one big bone, hissing, *"Sheeshee, sheeshee, sheeshee."* He picked up another,
grunted, and returned it to its place.

There was no sound from the circle of natives staring
at the spectacle. I desperately wanted to clear my throat
but restrained myself, having heard that it was a sign of
weakness. The *sheeshee, sheeshee* hissing continued, be-
coming more and more ominous.

The witch doctor picked up two small bones, rattled
them in cupped hands, and threw them between my feet.
A muscle in my calf twitched but I kept my feet firm.
The spear shape in the bones curled and twisted before
my eyes, like a snake coming towards me.

Still hissing, but softly now, the witch doctor got up
and scrutinized the pattern of bones, first from one side,
then from the other, shook his head, and returned to his
place. The bones seemed to lean towards him as he moved.
He fumbled in his belt and produced a large pair of green-
tinted, pink-rimmed sunglasses. I relaxed, smiling at the
absurdity. He peered at the bones, returned the glasses
to his belt, and looked round slowly, then up at me. His
eyes were wide, fixed, and brilliant.

After a long pause he began muttering in a singsong,
first unintelligibly, then clearly enough to be heard if one
strained one's ears. "Dhlozi! Dhlozi! A dhlozi is in this

place." (A dhlozi is an ancestral spirit.) "The dhlozi came from the bush to this house. It came in the form of a great green snake, a mamba. The mamba saw the son of the white man. It came towards him and coiled up. The child of the white man spoke to it, and the dhlozi lifted up its head and opened its mouth and came closer. No one who is bitten by a mamba ever lives out the day, but this mamba did not bite. It opened its mouth as if to speak, then lay quiet. It gazed at the youth, then returned to the bush, looking back like someone leaving a dear friend. The young man had a gun on the table but he did not shoot the green snake. He spoke to it gently, as one speaks to an old and honored person."

He broke off, and the circle of men around us all exhaled together, like a little breeze.

I was cold all over, and more than a little frightened. The evening before, while I was sitting on the verandah waiting for my father to come out for his drink, a green snake had come out of the bush and had gone through the curious motions the witch doctor described. It was all just as he related, except that the snake was not a deadly green mamba; it was a grass snake. I had let it be, knowing that it was harmless and thinking it might deal with a few mice in the storeroom. How did the witch doctor know? There was no one about when the incident occurred, and I had told no one except my father.

The witch doctor resumed. "Who is this dhlozi? What does he seek?" He paused for a long silence. "When a man dies and is buried, his spirit remains in that place until the proper ceremonies are performed after a year. Is it not so?"

The circle assented in chorus, "It is so."

He went on. "The ceremonies send a man's spirit home; then he troubles no one. But a spirit who was not sent home is restless, and may take the form of a deadly snake, who will kill to show his anger. Is it not so?"

"It is so," the listeners confirmed.

"Who then is this dhlozi? Is it someone who died in the great shaking sickness when there were not enough living people left to bury the dead? Or perhaps it is the spirit of a man who was neglected by his sons and now comes seeking strangers who will help him to go home."

"It is Ntambo!" one of the laborers exclaimed.

"That is the truth!" cried another. "It is the spirit of Ntambo!"

Ntambo was a legendary hunter who killed two lions singlehanded and was then himself killed by the rest of the pride. The lions did not maul the body, but guarded it against hyenas and vultures until Ntambo's friends came looking for him. When King Mpande heard what had happened, he forbade Ntambo's relatives to hold funeral ceremonies, because the king himself was called the Lion, and he did not want praises recited for a lion killer. Ntambo's spirit was therefore never sent home. Ntambo's feat had taken place on a rocky knoll not far from where our farmhouse now stood; the knoll was called the Place of the Dying of Ntambo.

The witch doctor shuffled up close to me, asking, "Do the bones lie, child of a white man?"

I did not believe in ghosts, but I was not so sure about amadhlozi. To Zulus, ancestral spirits were as real as the ancestors themselves. And if the witch doctor knew in such detail about me and the snake, might he not know other things? I did not like it at all.

The witch doctor repeated, "Do the bones lie, Nkosane?" (Nkosane means Little Chief.)

Trying to keep my voice steady, I said, "There was a green snake here last night. I did not shoot it, because it would do no harm."

The natives looked at one another, then at me. "Hau! So you speak with amadhlozi, Nkosane. It is a wonderful thing," they said.

I was glad to see Charlie go off with the laborers for their midday meal. I was too shaken to eat my own lunch and was still pretty nervous when he called at the farmhouse on his way home.

He seemed equally nervous. "Please forgive me," he pleaded. "When I was divining I was carried away, but now I realize that you may not want it known that you are friendly with an ancestral spirit."

"How did you know about the snake?" I demanded.

He widened his eyes and opened his mouth to start muttering, then changed his mind. "If I do not tell you, the spirit of Ntambo will. Then you will say, 'Charlie thinks that because he can deceive simple people, he can also deceive someone who speaks with spirits.' So I will tell you now, before you find out in your own way. I knew the people here would expect me to do something clever, so yesterday I came secretly through the bush and hid near the laborers' huts, hoping that I would hear some small things in their talk that I could reveal today. That is how I saw you talking to the snake."

I laughed foolishly in relief. He politely laughed, too,

until I stopped. Then he said, conspiratorially, "You will not betray me?"

I gave the Zulu sign for swearing an oath. He put his palm against mine and said, very hesitantly and seriously, "Nkosane, I have never before seen such a thing, such a fearsome thing as a man talking to a dhlozi. It is only possible to do so if there is a great bond between you and him. What did you say to the dhlozi?"

"I said, 'Snakey, snakey, what are you up to?' "

"Why did you talk to the mamba in English? How could he understand?"

"I thought it was a grass snake."

"You are very brave to talk familiarly to a dhlozi. What do those English words mean?"

"They mean, 'What do you want, little snake?' "

"What did the snake reply?"

"It stuck out its tongue but it did not make any sounds."

"Perhaps it would have answered if you had spoken Zulu. What are those words you said?"

"I said, 'Snakey, snakey . . .' "

"I see you do not want to tell me. Well, that is as it should be. Speaking with a dhlozi is not a trick. It is a fearful and dangerous gift, which a man must keep to himself. But remember: a dead man's spirit does not take the form of a deadly mamba if he is at peace."

"I thought it was a grass snake," I repeated.

"If you address him as Ntambo and speak Zulu, perhaps he will answer. But who am I to instruct *you* in such a matter?"

When Charlie went round the corner to fetch his baboon, I slipped the magnifying glass into his bag of divining bones. He left, begging me again to speak to the snake in Zulu, and warning me that a mamba bite is fatal.

When my father returned that evening I told him about the bone throwing and what Charlie had said. I did not tell him that Charlie had confessed to seeing the snake and hearing me talk to it; after all, I had promised not to betray Charlie. My father dismissed the part about Ntambo, but was intrigued by Charlie's knowing about the snake. Could it be telepathy? Perhaps while I concentrated on the bones I was unconsciously transmitting? For many years afterwards he and neighbors discussed whether it was extrasensory perception or telepathy or magic. They vied with one another in retelling stories about Charlie. He had told Abercrombie to look for his missing ox in the butcher's slaughterhouse, which was where it was. He had refused even to talk to Venter's wife, telling her to hurry back home: she got there in time to be with Venter when he died. Though the tales were nearly all to Charlie's credit, the neighbors disapproved of my father's letting me get mixed up in such dark native things. He said he could not stop me; the best he could do was to make sure I went to church once a month and changed my underwear regularly.

The snake returned next evening when the laborers were lined up to be paid, so they all saw it. It came straight towards me and coiled up a yard from my feet.

I said, "Snakey, snakey, what are you looking for?"

An old laborer called low and urgently, "Speak Zulu! Speak Zulu!"

I said in Zulu, "Ntambo, old father, we see you."

The snake lifted up its head and waited for what seemed a long time.

"Does he want to go home?" the laborer prompted.

"Do you want to go home, grandfather?" I asked.

The snake dropped its head, lifted it again, and gazed around; then dropped down and slithered into a hole in the floorboards.

"He agreed!" the laborers cried. "Did you ever hear of such a wonderful thing? Did you see the snake lift his head and bow it in agreement?"

Next morning a carelessly driven farm truck hit a calf, which had to be destroyed. One of the older laborers, who was skilled in such matters, stabbed it with a spear in the way that is right for a sacrifice. They sent for Charlie, who came and cut off snippets of spleen, heart, rumen, gall, and neck muscle, which he boiled up with herbs. All the men dipped their fingers in the concoction and sucked them. Then they stripped naked, put on token shirts made of rushes, and went up to the Place of the Dying of Ntambo to perform the ceremonies that should have been performed eighty years earlier to send home Ntambo's spirit.

For several weeks I kept watch for the snake, thinking that if I sat quiet on the verandah in the dusk it might reappear, but it never did.

Bloodsong

THE PATH OF THE ANCIENTS started somewhere on the tableland, where the clan chief, Insimbi, had his kraal, and it ran through the valley to the east hills, where many of the clansmen lived.

Our farm was part of the white settlement that lay in the valley dividing the clan's land. Natives crossing from one side to the other usually went by government road, but occasionally someone would use the Path of the Ancients. If my father saw him, or her, he would scold, pointing crossly to the sign NO TRESPASSERS. NO RIGHT OF WAY. He had had it translated into Zulu, but since the trespassers could not read, this made little difference, except that the place where the sign stood came to be called the Place of Scolding.

Sometimes a man, though more often an obstinate old woman, would insist on proceeding. My father fumed but did not otherwise interfere. "I suppose they have a right-of-way by immemorial usage," he said, in extenuation of his weakness. The path was not in fact im-memorial. All members of the clan knew exactly when it had been established. It had come into use nine gen-erations ago, when Duma of the Battleaxe had led the clan's ancestors down from the mountains to occupy this piece of thornveld. Every man, and almost every boy, could recite his own pedigree step by step back to Duma or one of his band. When you wanted to thank someone, or show respect, you called him Duma or Child of Duma.

I knew about the Path and Duma and Insimbi because Ngumbane, the foreman, was my friend. When things had gone wrong with my birth, Ngumbane had run fif-teen miles to fetch a doctor. The doctor arrived too late to save my mother, and the desperate run left Ngumbane with a permanent limp. My father gave him a Friesian cow in recompense. The affair also left Ngumbane with a permanent stake in my development. As soon as I could toddle, he began taking me on his rounds with him. He talked to me about animals and insects, the clan's history, farm activities, and the private lives of the farm laborers. For a long time I was more fluent in Zulu than in English, but when I learned to read I would translate bits of the newspapers to him. My father was happy about the re-lationship. He knew I was in safe and affectionate hands, and that left him free to go away on his hunting trips.

When I was fifteen, my father went off on an extended trip during my school holidays. I stayed on the farm, as usual. One Saturday afternoon, shortly before work stopped, Ngumbane said, "Nkosane, there is something we must talk about." When no other people were present, Ngumbane called me "my little boy" or Child of Duma

or perhaps by a fanciful praise-name describing my al-
leged feats or character traits: Mastiff That Breaks the
Dog Chain, Exterminator of Locusts, Shield That Pro-
tects Ngumbane from Wrath. His addressing me respectfully as Nkosane signaled something weighty. I sat down,
to show I recognized that he wanted a serious discussion.

"Nkosane," he said, "you know that the Paramount
Chief, whom we call the Lion, the chief of all our nation,
comes next month to visit Insimbi. All the clans around
here will meet to give him a royal greeting." I knew, of
course; it was a major topic of local news.

Ngumbane went on, "There will be war dances, as in
the old days. But the young men do not know all the
dances. They have never performed together in regiments, only in little bands. So there will be a gathering
tomorrow at Insimbi's place for them to practice together.
They do not want to be clumsy when they greet the Lion.
Many will come from over there." He pointed to the east
hills and paused, as if the implication were clear.

I said, "I am listening, my father."

He resumed, patiently. "Exterminator of Locusts, those
people who live over there must cross the valley to get
to Insimbi's place. They say that because it is for the honor
of the Lion, they will use the Path of the Ancients, as in
the old days, before there were white farms here."

I said, "That does not matter. I will give permission
to all who ask."

Ngumbane looked at his feet. "They will not ask,
Johnny. Some of the older men think they should, but
not the young ones. The youngsters say this day will be
as in the days of our grandfathers, when the clan could

pass freely over their own land. They are full of insolence.''

"What do you want me to do?" I asked.

"Why do you not go and visit the white village tonight?" he suggested. "If you are not here, the people
will cross over tomorrow morning and return tomorrow
night. If you are not here, their offense will not be seen,
and there will be no trouble."

I had no intention of going to spend a boring Sunday
in the village. "The people will be on the Path," I said.
"I shall stay here at the house. They will not see me, and
so they will not be uncomfortable, and I will pretend not
to know that they are there. After all, one cannot see the
Path from the house."

Ngumbane sighed and then nodded reluctantly. "That
will be good. Stay well, Johnny." He went off to join
the laborers, who had already lined up, ready to leave for
the African reserve where they had their homes.

I always enjoyed Sundays alone on the farm. On week-
days the dawn was full of the noises of oxen and mule
teams, carts creaking and drivers shouting. On Sundays,
in the quiet, one could hear successive waves of chirps
and singing from awakening birds and other small creatures. But this Sunday morning the bird sounds were
overlaid by something else — a pervasive hum, like that
of large, distant beehives. I could see nothing around the
house, so I took binoculars and climbed a tall lookout
tree that gave a view across the farmlands to the river
and the hills.

The Path of the Ancients, hardly noticeable in the normal course of events, was now thronged with an almost

unbroken line of people: men carrying oxhide shields and fighting sticks and capped with widow bird and ostrich plumes, and parties of women and girls in beads and ocher, carrying beer pots and food trays on their heads. All the way to the east hills little tributary trails fed more people into the thickening stream on the Path itself.

I had never seen such a sight. It would, of course, be even more spectacular when they and scores of other streams of people met at Insimbi's kraal. Why shouldn't I go there and see?

I quickly saddled a horse. I thought of wearing my riding breeches but decided against it: they would make me look like an official. Better to go in ordinary khaki pants. I stuffed some sandwiches into one saddlebag, and a few sticks of tobacco and boxes of matches into the other, for use as gifts. My eye fell on a large gray pebble; I added it, to throw on the cairn that flanked the Path. I set off along the farm road, which ran from the farmhouse over a little ridge. Beyond the ridge it briefly joined the Path.

The Path itself, usually no more than overgrown track obliterated in parts by ploughing, was now sharply defined by the passage of many feet. It meandered to avoid obstacles that no longer existed, curved wide round a marsh long since drained, and twisted between circular patches marking places where trees had once stood.

The marchers resolutely followed the Path's original route, never taking a shortcut, even where the Path ran across a ploughed field or sown pasture.

I waited for a break in the line. Several times people obligingly stopped, saying, "So you're coming with us," but I waved them on, because I knew the horse would be an embarrassment in the middle of a group. Some marchers greeted me, or saluted, or remarked on the horse. Twice a woman called, "Ha, Sea-eyes!" whereupon her companions all looked at me, saying, "Truly, eyes like the sea." Blue eyes never failed to amaze the Zulus.

The parties of older men marched stolidly, merely muttering a repetitive song phrase to keep time — "The strength of the antbear," "The bees of the mountain," "Kindle fire, my lads, kindle fire." The young men sang more elaborate part-songs or solemnly recited an old war song: "Shame on the man who is burned in his hut. Come out and fight."

Eventually a break in the line allowed me to get onto the Path. I intended to leave it farther on, where it diverged from the straighter farm road, but when I made to turn off, the man ahead of me put out his arm to stop the horse. "That is not the way," he said reprovingly. When we reached the NO TRESPASSERS sign at the Place of Scolding, a number of people turned round and looked at me, smiling, but no one said anything.

The line halted when we reached the stone cairn. It is very bad to pass one of these cairns without adding another stone to it; consequently, all stones for hundreds of yards around had been picked up. Prudent people avoided bad luck by bringing small stones with them if they were to pass this way. Most of the people ahead of me had remembered to bring pebbles, and duly threw them onto the pile, sometimes spitting on them first, but some had forgotten, and were now having to search the veld. When

I reached the stopping place and took my pebble out of
my saddlebag, I heard congratulatory shouting and laughter. A girl cried, "Did you bring a stone for me, too?"
An old woman reprimanded her for being pert to a white
man.

From here onward the Path climbed an escarpment,
winding round many bends. I had to dismount and lead
the horse. About halfway up, the marchers ahead stopped.
When we got moving again, I saw the cause. In a little
enclave beside the trail sat a skinny old man, with his leg
stretched out and a very twisted ankle. Some young men
were comforting him and lashing together sticks to make
a crutch. I said, "Can you ride a horse, grandfather?"

The old man grinned through his pain. "I have never
ridden a horse, Nkosane. Surely your white man's horse
will resent an old black man and throw me off?"

"No," I said reassuringly, "he is tame. He and I both
respect old age."

The old man laughed. The youths carefully lifted him
to put him on the saddle. Before scrambling over he
motioned for them to wait. He took off his leopardskin
cape and spread it meticulously over the saddle so that
he would not touch the leather with his bare legs. He said
quietly, apologetically, "We old folks smell," and then
settled on the saddle, gripped the pommel with one hand,
and waved with the other. "Look," he declared grandly.
"I am a mounted policeman. Salute the servant of the
government!" The crowd laughed and cursed happily,
enjoying the opportunity to jeer with impunity at a policeman, especially a mounted one.

A boy came forward to take the reins, but I waved him

aside. "Never let a stranger touch your reins" was one of my father's rules. I led the horse up the hill, feeling very foolish. No white person was likely to see me, leading a horse like a servant, with a crowing old Zulu in the saddle; but you never know, so I kept my head down.

When we reached the top of the hill, the young men pointed out a kraal close by. We took the old man there. He praised me excessively. "Duma!" he shouted. "Chief of Chiefs! May you grow like a mountain!" I wished him well and headed for Insimbi's place.

Outside the kraal, on the level tableland, I saw hundreds of men. They were forming into companies, most of them with matching shields — black, or black and white, or white, or brown and white. Some companies were in single or double files, stamping to the rhythm of their own chants. Graybeards with long sticks demonstrated songs and steps, shouted orders, and whacked the shins of men who stepped out of line.

I gave the main crowd a wide berth and rode round to the back of the kraal. I halted twenty yards or so from the stockade and waited. A small boy playing there leapt to his feet, shouting, "White man! There is a white man!" Some women peered curiously. Presently a man appeared. He was obviously someone of importance. I dismounted and saluted him. He acknowledged my greeting and then asked, anxiously, "What is the matter, child of a white man? Is there trouble? Why have you come?"

I explained that I wanted to see the dancing. Would the chief please allow me? I presented the twists of tobacco.

He took the tobacco and smelled it approvingly. "You

have a great liver," he said, "to come into our country, black people's country, on a day like this. But you know how to show respect. Where did you learn Zulu?"

I told him about Ngumbane. "The limping one," he said. "He used to be a fine dancer. I will tell the chief you are here. Take your horse over there." He pointed to a tree beyond a little ravine. "It will be a safe place, but do not offsaddle."

I dismounted under the tree and gave the horse his nosebag. Presently two little girls appeared, one carrying a small pot of beer, the other a grass mat with a lump of meat. I gave them sandwiches in exchange.

As the day wore on, the drilling on the tableland grew more and more orderly. The smaller companies were amalgamating into regiments, performing maneuvers in long waves. They advanced slowly; charged, beating their shields; retreated; advanced again; repeating the exercises until their elderly instructors were satisfied or exhausted.

By early afternoon the exercises were breaking up. Women had for some time been carrying out food and beer, and most of the dancers now sat down, quiet except for an occasional showoff who leapt about, slashing and stabbing at an imaginary enemy. A few real fights had also broken out, and some spectators were trying to stop them; others were excitedly urging on the combatants or joining in. The chief and other older men were having to intervene, shouting and laying about them with clubs and whips.

Glancing at the group around Insimbi, I saw several arms pointing to me. Soon afterwards a youth of about my age appeared. He was bleeding from a head wound and had a weal where a whip had got him. He stood provocatively in front of me and said, "Little white man" — he used an insulting diminutive — "little white man, hear the words of the chief. Insimbi says you must go now. He says in the dusk a white man looks like any other wild creature."

I mounted quickly. "I thank the chief," I said. "I send him respects." I added, condescendingly, "Stay well, little lad," and cantered off.

Many of the women and girls had already left, together with older men who were anxious to reach home before dark. They started off in big groups, which shed fragments as family or neighborhood parties broke off to go their separate ways. No one made way for me. A group of men stood in front of the horse and demanded that I take one of them to ride with me; I had to make a wide detour to get past them. Several times someone said, "What are you doing here, white man?" Once or twice a man deliberately tried to frighten the horse.

I decided not to risk the Path of the Ancients down the escarpment; there were too many little danger points. Instead, I went a long way round on the government road and did not get home until after sunset. A few stragglers were still on the Path, but the main traffic had apparently passed.

I finished supper and was getting ready for bed when my horse became restless. I had tethered him for the night in a little cornfield near the house. The dead cornstalks had been gathered into bundles, which stood like rows of ghostly men in the moonlight. The horse was so disturbed that I feared a predator might be around. Then I heard what had been disturbing him. It was far away but unmistakable: a war song, sung by a great many men. It sounded like a whole regiment.

I had already undone the tether and let the horse canter off before I realized that I now had no means of getting away if I needed to.

The sound came and then went faint. It was an antiphonal song, the leading voices clear and high, the responses muffled but strong. It grew suddenly louder. By visualizing the Path of the Ancients, I could tell how the sound would alter. As the singers went down through the old riverbed, it faded; it grew louder as they emerged, and faded again as they went around the hillock at the Place of Scolding. When they reached the ridge opposite the farmhouse, the sound should almost disappear.

After a moment's silence, too soon for them to have reached the ridge, a new song started, a different sound. I could not hear words, and indeed the song had no words: just *Eee yoh haa haa haa,* starting quiet, rising high almost to a scream, and then falling to the deepest guttural that the singers could reach in their throats and chests. High again, then down, down, *haa! haa!* High, then down low, repeated over and over.

I knew the song, because a gang of laborers on the farm had once started singing it. Ngumbane had intervened, very angry, shouting, "We will have no songs like that here!" He told me it was a song that had been sung in the old days when warriors anticipated a great killing. "When you sing it, your blood wants blood," he said. In my mind I called it the Bloodsong.

The sound receded when the singers got to where the

Path ran behind the ridge, and grew faint as they went down into the old stone quarry. I went indoors with much relief: they were on their way to the hills. Then a great burst of the Bloodsong hit me. A large company of warriors had silently climbed the ridge and was now massing at the head of the clearing that ran down to the house. Obviously the others, on the Path, had gone on singing to provide a cover so that this party could get close to the farmhouse without being detected.

As fast as I could, I shuttered the windows and locked all the doors except the top half of the kitchen door. I put the pressure lamp to shine out through the door, dragged sacks of meal and seeds to form a little barricade, and loaded both barrels of the shotgun. I put in birdshot, because that was what I mostly used, but then I remembered that when the farmers had formed a commando to get the madman who shot his wife and kids, they all loaded up with slugs or buckshot, so I quickly slipped in buckshot instead.

In the moonlight I could see the great shields of the warriors gleam when they turned. They were now singing the battle challenge: "Shame on the man who is burned in his hut. Come out and fight!" As they sang, they shuffled into some kind of formation. I knew what they would do: they would split into three lots to form the bull, the classical Zulu attack formation. The two horns of the bull advance to harass the enemy's flanks while the main body, the bull's chest, awaits the right moment for a frontal charge. My father's friends had not been in the Zulu wars, but they often talked about them; their theory was that if you managed to crumple one of the bull's horns, the whole force was thereby confounded. One had therefore to concentrate on one horn and bring down as many men in it as possible.

Presently two files of men, rather fewer than I had expected, began creeping down the clearing. I tried to gauge the distance — not easy in the moonlight — and desperately wished I could remember what the *Sportsman's Handbook* said about the range, penetration, and scatter pattern of buckshot. As one horn moved diagonally across the clearing, I cocked both hammers and kept my bead on the leader, wondering whether I should aim at his legs or at his chest. If I only wounded him, perhaps the others would not be deterred. But what if I killed him?

I was puzzled, because the two horns were not advancing to surround the house but were moving obliquely towards the cornfield. The singing of the main body suddenly stopped. After a thin scream of command they all charged, shouting and hissing the clan battle cry. I scrambled out of the kitchen into the storeroom, which gave a view of that side of the clearing. I doubted whether I could get set up in there before they had me. I tore open the window shutter and pushed the gun barrels out, ready for the first man who came within range.

No one was there. But in the cornfield the whole company was stabbing and slashing at the upright bundles of stalks, crying, "Die! Die!" or leaping about in shadow combat with unseen enemies. I felt a great warm wetness down my trousers as I shakily put the gun down.

The display in the cornfield lasted only a few minutes. Soon most of the warriors sat down, breathing heavily.

I counted only a dozen or fifteen of them. One man walked to the house, deliberately standing in the lamplight. He leaned his shield and sticks against the wall and stood waiting, making a knocking click with his tongue.

I shouted, "What do you want?" immensely relieved that my voice was rough and harsh, not fearful and squeaky. The man saluted in the direction of my voice. I saw that he was a boy, not much older than I was. "Nkosane, we ask for water. We are dying of thirst," he said.

I replied gruffly, "Wait. I am coming," and frantically looked for a pair of trousers to replace my wet ones. I unloaded the shotgun, alarmed to see how shaky my hands were. Then I went out, unlocked the water tank, and gave the youth a tin mug.

He waved to the others. They carefully stacked shields and sticks against the wall and respectfully greeted me. They were all teenagers. Each one drank in turn, taking care not to spill. The last one rinsed the mug and held it over his head, looking at me for permission. I said, "You would not do that if it were beer." They recognized my weak joke as a gesture and laughed uproariously, boasting about their drinking capacities.

I waited for them to go, but they sat down, obviously intending to rest and talk. One youth said, "Nkosane, did you know that old man with the broken ankle?" I recognized the speaker and two of the others as having been among those assisting the old man. I shook my head. He turned to the group and related what had happened. They appeared to know already, for two of them were miming the old man putting down his cape to protect the saddle. Everyone laughed, and someone said, "He smells like a polecat's backside now, but they say he was a great fighter when he was young." Someone else said, "You did a kind thing, Nkosane. Our little band has come to thank you. That old man is greatly honored in our family. He was the guardian uncle of my father and of this boy's father." He indicated another youth, who seemed to be the leader. The leader said, "Johnny, you took a thorn from the foot of a stranger. So we give you this praise-name: You Pull Out Thorns for Strangers." The rest applauded, drummed on their shields, and cried "Thorn Puller," "You Pull Out Thorns." We discussed praise-names and the uncomplimentary nicknames of some of the white farmers. My father was called the Dancer, because he stamped his feet when he was angry.

I went into the house and brought out a big tin of rusks and some tobacco. They demolished the food and made rough cigarettes. They asked if I was courting. I fetched a picture of my girlfriend. They stared at it, carefully not touching with their fingers but holding it on open palms, and exclaimed admiringly at her plumpness.

They showed me a big stone axe they had found in a cliff in the hills. They had had it ritually purified in case it had been used to kill a man; the old women said that small yellow cannibals used to live in those cliffs. They asked whether I had not been scared up at Insimbi's, being the only white person there. The boys who had been with the old man said, "We kept an eye on you where you sat under the tree. If any trouble had started, we would have protected you." The leader assented. "With brave men like us you would have been safe. Did you see us attack that enemy in the cornfield? They outnumbered us many times, but we slew them without mercy. We were heroes, were we not?" There was much laughter as various members of the band enacted their own past or future exploits. I fetched the shield Ngumbane had given me. They examined and admired it, and I had a mock stick fight with one of them; several gave me advice or demonstrated cunning blows and feints.

The moon was sinking towards the western tableland before they left. As they went by, each one said, "Stay well, brother," and clasped me by the forearm. Then they all turned round and cried, "Puller of Thorns! You are one of us," and raised their shields in salute. For the next half hour I could hear their voices, clear and soaring *Eee yoh,* then falling low, deep and ominous, *haa haa haa.* The Bloodsong faded, rose, faded, and finally died in the valleys of the east hills.

I often saw members of the band subsequently, loafing around trading stores, working on farms, or trotting down the highway to the music of a mouth organ. They always greeted me with the greatest friendliness, but none of them ever again called me brother or said, "You are one of us."

Incident at
Mhlaba Jail

VISITORS often stopped to take pictures of the jail parking area, with its big central oval of dark green grass and trees, and the black convicts in their red shirts meticulously pulling up small weeds one by one. The convicts chattered quietly or hummed little songs in unison, giving an impression of peace and of men contented with their gentle occupation. There was rarely much traffic, but this Saturday morning three farm trucks were parked across one end of the tarmac, and a little group of white men stood near the jail gate, admiring a sheet of plywood propped against a two-by-four. On it, in luminous orange paint, was the legend NKULU RECEPTION COMMITTEE. I stopped on the opposite side of the road and leaned out to see what was going on.

Ronnie Roland's leopardskin cap stood out above the heads of the other men. He waved. "Hallo, Jim. Come and see my new burdizzo. On the double, now, Corporal. Lef' ri', lef' right.

The others joined in sycophantically. "Lef' right. Come
on, Corp, lef' ri'.

We had all been together in the army ten years earlier
on the Angola border, in 27 Squad (Special Duties). Ronnie had been our sergeant — a good sergeant — and he
liked to remind us of it by using our military ranks and
by buying the first round and the last round whenever
he met any of us at the bar. "Sergeant's privilege," he
would explain, smiling but steely-eyed, brooking no argument.

I parked and walked across. Ronnie flourished a big
stainless steel instrument, like a pair of pincers with wide
jaws and a complicated double joint. He picked a thick
twig off a hibiscus shrub, put it between the instrument's
jaws, pushed the handles together, then released them
and held up the twig in triumph.

"See, the core is cut through but the bark is undam-
aged. Clever, eh? Invented by a cunning old Italian veterinary, Dr. Burdizzo."

"Whatever for?"

"Bloodless castrater, Jim boy. Fit the top of the ram's
testicle in here, press the handle, and thip! the cord's cut.
It's the vas deferens, I believe. Same for the other testicle.
The tube's cut but the skin's intact. No wound, no in-
fection, but the ram can't ram no more. Yes, sir," he
sang, "he ain't gonna ram no more, no more, he ain't
gonna ram no more."

"Only today it's not a sheep," Piet Smuts said. "It's a
big black buck. A sable antelope, you could say. Eh, that's
witty, man, isn't it? A sable antelope is a black buck. Get
it? When they release Nkulu through the jail gate, here

we shall be, waiting to meet and greet him. Surprise! Surprise! Eh? I can't wait to see his face."

"It's not his face I'm after," Bill said.

He and the rest of the reception committee demonstrated how they would pull a grain bag over Nkulu's head, gag him, tie his ankles, and rip open his trousers for Ronnie to use the burdizzo. "From the time he emerges till the exercise is over will be one minute, forty-three seconds, you'll see. Precision commando operation, like old Twenty-seven Squad. Want to join us, Jim? Actually we don't need another man, but you could take pictures for the record. Show those girls what we go through to protect them. Use my camera; I've just put in a new roll of film."

"Hell, chaps," I said. "You can't do this. It's a bloody criminal assault. And the fellow's innocent."

"Well, why did they arrest him, then?" David Barnard demanded.

"They made a mistake," I said. "Mrs. Oosthuizen is now certain it was not Nkulu."

"I thought she said it was too dark to see. So how can she be sure it wasn't him?" Piet asked triumphantly.

Bill clicked the burdizzo's jaws next to my ear. "Say, why do you care so much about this Bantu? Is he a buddy of yours? You don't want to be known as the friend of a native rapist, Jim. But I'd do the same if he was white." He clicked the burdizzo again.

I snatched ineffectually at the instrument. "I don't have to be his friend to be against your sadism," I said. "It's bloody pathological."

"Ooh, long words," Dave said. "And they're insulting, too, I'll bet."

"Watch it, Jim," Ronnie interrupted. "You'll get these
fellows all worked up and wanting to practice on you."
He gave a face-contorting wink and took me by the arm.
"Come on, Jim. We know you don't like rough games."

He walked me resolutely across the road. "Jim, lad,
we've got to keep the squad going." He shifted his hand
to my shoulder. "Once men have seen action together,
danger and death and blood together, like you and I and
the other chaps have, there's a bond, Jim. It's the old
comrades' ésprit, and we've got to preserve it. You know
as well as I do a few drunk-ups don't do it. It needs
something that will get the old adrenaline moving. Like
today's little affair." He opened my door for me. "Remember, Jim, once a comrade, always a comrade."

"Sure, Ronnie. But how can you sacrifice this poor
bloody native? He didn't do anything!" I could hear my
voice going high and a little hysterical.

He laughed his warm, deep laugh. "I bet he would
have done it if he'd had the chance. I wouldn't mind
giving Betty Oosthuizen a feel-up myself." He poked a
finger in my ribs and left.

A number of white passersby stopped at the reception
committee placard, where Piet and Ronnie described what
they were going to do. There were scandalized giggles
and shrieks from women as the burdizzo was held up and
explained. Now and then there was a male squawk, when
Ronnie playfully lunged the instrument at a man's crotch.
Meantime, the rest of the reception committee did a few
rehearsal drills, manhandling one of their number to the

ground and getting busy with gags and ropes. They looked like a first-aid class playing a game.

A few natives also paused, but the reception committee ushered them on, saying courteously, "No, boy," or "No, my friend, this not for you." Most natives left, but some merely moved across the road, asking one another what was happening. Then there was a sudden murmur of anger, and a boy sprinted down the road to where a native road gang was at work. They followed him back, carrying their crowbars and pickaxes.

Their induna, or leader, ducked into the scrub at the roadside and emerged beside my truck, where he could not be seen by the reception committee. He was a heavy, villainous-looking man, with a long scar down his cheek and across his mouth.

"Baas," he said in a deep whisper.

"Yes, boy, what is it? Do I know you?"

He said, tentatively, in Zulu, "Baas. It is said baas is a friend of Nkulu."

"I know him slightly. We have met at meetings."

"It is said you are a friend."

I did not reply. He waited a few seconds and then said, "I have never spoken with him."

I remained silent.

"Baas Jim," he said. "We do not want to make a procession to walk down the street with Nkulu as if he is a great chief. We want only to let him get away before Baas Roland can do a bad thing to him. To take away his manhood! A man's manhood is the seed of his tribe."

"It is a matter for the police," I said firmly.

He ignored my remark. "The door in the jail gate

always opens at nine o'clock. My men and I will be there. When they let Nkulu out, we shall seize him and hustle him over here into your truck. You must be ready to drive off before Baas Roland and his friends can get here. But in any case we shall stand guard till you are off."

"I don't want to get mixed up in this affair. It is not my business," I said. "And it is not yours. Leave it."

He answered patiently, "Baas, God sent you to this place, on this day, when you are needed, and God put me and my gang close by, where we could find out what Baas Roland means to do. Also, think: if Nkulu is hurt, there will be deaths in this village tonight. Then the other white people will ask, Why did Baas Jim not help Nkulu get away?"

"It is a matter for the police," I repeated.

"The police know all about Nkulu. If they wanted him to be safe, then they would be here. But the police are not here. Baas Roland is here, with his shiny iron castrater. So my gang and our crowbars must be the policemen. You will be safe, baas. No one argues with ten crowbars. I put down your tailgate now so that we can throw Nkulu in without pausing, like a bag of grain." He sidled to the rear of the truck and let the flap down. "Start your motor, baas, *brrm, brrm*. It is nearly nine o'clock."

"No!" I insisted. "I am not going to help you. You are making trouble. Big trouble."

"Start your motor, baas!" the induna hissed urgently. "If we do not succeed there will be bloodshed today."

I started the motor. The induna said, "That is good," like an adult praising a child. He made his way back through the bushes and reappeared, leading his men across the road and over the forecourt to the jail gate. They lined up opposite Ronnie's committee. The spectators had drifted away, and so the two groups had the forecourt to themselves.

I got out of my cab to watch, leaving the door open and the motor running for a quick getaway.

Piet Smith addressed the road gang politely — "Move away, please. We need this space" — and motioned with his arm.

The gang did not move.

He turned to the induna. "Shift your gang, please, induna."

The induna said impassively, "We have work here, baas."

"You can go in when we have finished. We shall not be long," Piet said, a little impatiently.

"Our work is here." The induna pointed at the asphalt in front of his feet, and spat, as if to mark the spot.

"What work? I don't see any work."

"Come on, you kaffirs, get to work!" the induna growled.

One of the gang broke into a work song. "Ma-simtate! Simti! Nyigiti!" The others joined in, chanting very slowly. They bent down, miming intense effort, as if their crowbars were part of a heavy beam. "Si-i-imti," they groaned, swinging the phantom beam back, then "Nyigiti" as they swung it forward.

"Goddam insolence," Piet swore.

"Simti," the gang intoned. "Simti. Nyigiti."

We had all heard the song scores of times, at railway

sidings, factories, construction sites. After five or six "simti"s the gang would have established a team rhythm; then the song leader would yell, "Shaaa-ya!" and they would heave the load up to wherever it was to go. We tensed, expecting the song leader to give the word, but he went on stolidly chanting with the rest, "Simti. Nyigiti. Simti. Nyigiti."

"Get on with it, man," Dave Barnard muttered. "Say 'Shaya,' man. Say 'Shaya.'"

The gang maintained its slow beat. "Simti. Nyigiti."

"Christ, Ronnie," Bill said. "You didn't say anything about this. I didn't bring a sidearm or anything. We'd better get some wrenches and tire levers out of the trucks, man."

"We're not in Angola now. No violence unless we're attacked," Ronnie commanded. "Just stand your ground, boys. We'll be fine."

"This isn't what I came for," Dave Barnard complained. "You know I can't afford trouble right now, Ronnie. I'm on a suspended, man. If I get in trouble I go inside for twelve months. Twelve months! And my wife's expecting." He was almost screaming. "She's expecting!"

"There won't be any trouble," Ronnie said. "Just remember your unarmed combat, boys. But we won't blame you if you skip out, Dave."

"It's not what I came for!" Dave cried. "It's not fair!"

"Okay, Dave, okay," Piet said. "But don't howl in front of the . . . the" — he struggled for a word — "the other people, eh."

The road gang's chant was speeding up and they were now rhythmically stamping their feet as if starting a war dance. "Simti, nyigiti, simti, nyigiti, nyigiti, simti, nyi-giti. Eee-yoh!" The induna stood aloof, silent, watching Ronnie. Piet Smuts took his hunting knife from the sheath on his belt, looked at it, and put it back, keeping his hand on it with the flap unbuttoned.

"Might as well abort, with this mob around," Bill said.

"Can't back down now," Ronnie replied. "Everybody in town would know by lunchtime."

Suddenly the induna gave a high double whistle. The gang stopped singing and stood still. The door in the jail gate creaked and opened. The induna and Piet Smuts craned forward, their heads almost touching. A native guard came out; he hesitated at the sight of so many men around him, then continued forward, followed by ten or twelve native convicts carrying garden trowels. They walked nervously down the path between the road gang and the committee. Another native guard began closing the door, but Ronnie put his boot in it.

"Where's Nkulu?" he demanded. The guard held the door hard against Ronnie's boot and apparently signaled someone. A white warder appeared.

"You're obstructing a prison officer in the course of his duty, Mr. Roland," he said. "What do you think you're doing?"

"Where's Nkulu?" Ronnie demanded again.

"I believe a prisoner was taken by the police and set free somewhere else during the night."

"The bloody bastards!" Ronnie shouted. "The low-down, deceiving bastards!"

"He's lying. They've got him in there!" Piet Smuts

cried, trying to push in past the native guard. The warder slapped his pistol holster angrily. "I've never yet shot a man who was trying to break *into* prison. But there's always a first time, eh. What business is Nkulu of yours, anyway?" He kicked Ronnie's foot out of the way and viciously slammed the steel door.

The induna relayed to his men what the warder had said. "Is it true?" he asked the native guard. The guard confirmed it: the police had had a special paper from the magistrate, saying they were to release Nkulu in the native reserve at dawn.

The induna shouted, "Nkulu has gone. He is safe. The affair is over," and gestured his men to follow him. He carefully avoided looking in my direction and made a small detour to go past the reception committee's vehicles. As he passed Ronnie's truck he dropped his crowbar on the vehicle's immaculate wing, denting it and cracking off a long streak of paint. "Sorry, baas," he said. "Very sorry." Each of the laborers dropped or scraped a tool on a truck as he went by, and said, "Excuse, please, master," or "Sorry, my baas."

By the time Ronnie's party had ended their mutual jeers, mocking laughter, and recriminations, the road gang was back at work as if nothing had happened.

One day six months after the incident, the induna waved me down a few miles out of the village.

"Are you well, Jim?" ("Jim," I noticed, not "Baas Jim.") "I bring praises from Nkulu. I told him he is only a man whom you used to meet at meetings, but he persists that you are a friend. He could not risk being seen in the white village, and so he could not personally thank you for leading the rescue party at the jail.''

"I did no such thing, and you know it," I protested.

He shrugged. "It is what is being said among black people. It cheers some of the old ones. Of course, my men and I are heroes, too. The lion makes the kill, but the jackals also get to share the meat." He smiled an evil grin, showing broken teeth where the scar cut across his lip. "When I am asked if you are a friend of mine, I reply, 'No, we are battle comrades.' That is so, is it not?"

Death of
the Nation

In my boyhood every small white boy on a farm in Natal had a black companion, an umfaan. The umfaan was usually three or four years older than the white boy so that he could take care of his charge and carry him piggyback when necessary. My umfaan was called Fakwes. His real name was Ukufakwezwe, "Death of the Nation," because he was born at the time of an epidemic that killed a great many people, including his father.

He was ten or eleven when he came to work on my family's farm, which meant that he had had five or six years as a herd boy, spending all day every day in the veld with the other boys of his family. He knew the name of every bird, every little animal, even every insect, we came across, and he knew what one should do about each of them — which bees sting and which merely buzz, how to salute the praying mantis, and what to cry out to the nightjar when it suddenly flies up and then flops down, invisible in deep shadow. (You say, "Savolo, savolo, milk for my people.")

We collected quails' eggs, flying ants, and small white tubers and roasted them on the lid of a cast-iron pot. We hunted cane rats and lizards and helped herd the cattle. Sometimes we went with one of Fakwes's relatives to visit the native reserve adjoining the farm. We took salt, tobacco, and matches as gifts, and perhaps a beer bottle of lard, liquid in the heat. We were received ceremoniously, like adults, and when Fakwes's grandfather took the tobacco, he invited us into his hut, which was very special because of his spears and his big oxhide shield.

An exciting thing happened on one of those visits. On our way home we heard a shout from very far away, then a louder one close by from a man high in a tall tree. He was shouting, "The goats are in the field!" Fakwes ran to a big tree, climbed up, and shouted the same words. Someone picked up the message, and we could hear it repeated from the next hilltop and then the next, far away.

"Where are the goats?" I demanded. "Shouldn't we run and chase them?"

"You will see the goats in a little while," he said. "They will be riding horses and carrying revolvers."

Some time afterwards — I think we had ridden more than a mile — the "goats" appeared. They were two policemen on horseback. Fakwes said that by the time they reached the kraals all the men who did not have passes or poll-tax receipts would be hiding in deep bush, together with all the unlicensed dogs.

"You have seen a secret thing," he said. "You must never speak of it." He knew that if he said it was secret

I would not tell, just as I did not tell when we killed the prize rooster with our catapults. I never did tell, though I felt guilty and anxious whenever a policeman looked directly at me, in case he knew.

My first few school years were in a one-roomer a few miles from our place. I rode a pony to school; Fakwes walked or trotted alongside. Out of sight of adults we both rode, or Fakwes rode and I tried to keep up. When we reached the school, I went into the playground while Fakwes joined the other umfaans and the ponies in the school's field. The umfaans played games of guessing how many pebbles there were under which condensed-milk tin, breaking off to listen to our singing lessons. When we emerged, they would break into "John Peel" or "Land of Hope and Glory," rendering it loudly and perfectly but with a distinctive African flavor.

On the way home I regaled Fakwes with what I had learned that day. After lunch we usually went down to the reservoir to draw in the soft mud left by the receding water. (There must also have been times when the water was rising, but I don't remember them.) There were long, flat, absolutely smooth stretches of yellow ooze. Whatever one scratched on it stayed put while the mud dried and finally cracked into big flat pieces like gigantic slabs of chocolate. Fakwes drew bulls with enormous horns and genitals and cows with long teats. I drew faces and wrote letters. He laughed when I wrote FAKWES and said it was his name. In response he scratched zigzag lines and said they were my name, but after a while he took writing seriously and began to copy letters from my books. He was quicker and neater than I was. He wanted to write his whole, long, real name, but I could not cope with long words and we had to abandon it. He drew one of his fearsome bulls and said, "Let that be the writing for my name."

We had trouble with other Zulu words, because I did not know how to write the click sounds. The teacher said that Zulu was not made for writing, it was for savages; but by the time I left the one-roomer to go to Big School in the village, twenty miles away, Fakwes and I could both read the Zulu on the packets of baby formula at the trading store. It said that baby formula was better than milk.

Once I was at Big School, I saw Fakwes only when I came home on weekends. Though only fifteen or sixteen, he received a full man's wages, because he could read and write figures and work out piecework tasks and things like that. I brought him a Zulu New Testament, which was the only Zulu book I could find. He was ecstatic. "I shall be as clever as a preacher! I shall know all that he knows, from this Believers' book. But I will not be a Believer." He wrote me a careful letter of thanks in Zulu and signed it with one of his drawings of a bull.

The New Testament was full of place names — Nazareth, Bethlehem, Rome, Ephesus. But where were they? We went through my school atlas. What really gripped him in the atlas was England. He scoffed at the idea that such a small red patch could be the England that had defeated the Zulus, the Boers, and the Germans. His grandfather liked to tell how *his* father had fought at Isandhlwana, where the Zulus wiped out Lord Chelmsford's column, and at Ulundi, where the British broke the Zulus. The withered old man had a deep respect for British soldiers. "They were all heroes," he recounted. "They died without flinching. And they killed without flinching. Like Zulus." He enjoyed the little red-coated lead soldier I brought him, and attached it to the end of a spear.

Fakwes shared his grandfather's admiration for British soldiers but deeply resented settlers. "One day we will take back all this land," he declared. "We will burn the sugar cane and take the horses and cattle and sheep. The farmers will load their trucks and go, go south, away from us. I will be a great man in the council of chiefs, because I can read and I know where England is, and Bethlehem. I will write letters for the council of chiefs, and I will live in Armstrong's house." Armstrong, the storekeeper, had a place in the East Indian–colonial style, with little turrets and fretwork lattices, painted what we called coolie pink. "On letters to friends I will draw a bull. And you, my brother" — he put his arm around me — "you will be our adviser. The great chiefs always had a white man to tell them the thoughts and deceits of the English. We will give you many wives and red Boer cattle with their horns swept back, and a little band of warriors to guard you and greet you with praises. Which house would you like?"

One weekend when I came home, Fakwes was not there. No one knew where he was, and the police were looking for him. A youth with whom he had quarreled at a beer-drink had been found unconscious by the road-side, with a head wound. If he died, the police would probably charge Fakwes with murder. My father let it be known that we would arrange a lawyer if Fakwes turned himself in, but that proviso was unnecessary. The wounded youth recovered and refused to make a complaint — it was a fair fight, he said — and so no charge was recorded against Fakwes. Fakwes nevertheless stayed away. We heard rumors that he had been seen in Durban, and then in Cape Town. About a year after Fakwes disappeared, I received a card with a London postmark. It had a picture of a red-coated soldier. There was no message, only a drawing of a bull with big horns and genitals.

About five years ago I had a visit from Benny Miller. He was, and is, an undistinguished lawyer with a drinking problem. Most of his clients were shopkeepers charged with minor breaches of municipal bylaws, but he had also, surprisingly, appeared in two or three African political trials.

He phoned me one evening at my house. "I didn't want to be seen coming to your office," he said. "Your friends might think you were involved with one of my clients, and that wouldn't do, eh?"

"What do you want?" I snapped.

"I'm representing an old friend of yours. You may be able to help."

I agreed to see him, and within twenty minutes he arrived through the backyard servants' entrance. He was a plump, sallow man with curly gray hair and a practiced, self-deprecating smile. He accepted a drink, looked round the room, and remarked, "Nice place you have here."

I waited, not concealing my dislike.

"Do you know a man called Mkize? Big fellow, around forty."

I could not recall a black acquaintance by that name.

"He says to tell you the goats are in the field."

"Oh, Fakwes!" I exclaimed. I had forgotten that his clan name was Mkize. "Fakwes. Sure. We grew up together, but I haven't seen him for years. Where is he?"

"In jail. Forged papers and possession of an offensive weapon. But that's just to hold him until they get to the red meat. I think the prosecution is after conspiracy or sabotage or worse. He was abroad a long time and speaks fluent Portuguese and French."

"French! Fakwes speaks French?"

"Quite educated French, as far as I can judge. He seems to have got around."

"Portuguese and French, eh?" I could not believe it. "Well, how can I help?"

"Perhaps you can't help at all. But if there's no concrete evidence against him, just suspicion, then they might go for detention without trial. In that case character evidence may ease his lot. Someone like you — upright, prosperous, right wing — could carry weight, perhaps pull a string or two. I understand you have friends in government circles. Well, we all have our weaknesses. I should warn you, though, a dossier is bound to be opened for anyone who's connected with him."

"I'll think it over," I said.

He took it as a refusal. "I don't blame you. Things are never quite the same once you've been mixed up in one of these affairs."

"I'm not mixed up in anything," I protested.

"No? Consider this: you're a friend of a subversive character. He sent you a code message through me, which you obviously understood. Perhaps on your trips abroad you stopped over in Nairobi or Lourenço Marques or Marseilles, where he also happened, just happened, to be at the same time. Adds up. So you're probably wise to turn your back. Boyhood pals across the color line is one thing — touching, in fact — but in adults it's suspicious."

He rose to go, putting his glass down noisily. I held it up and looked inquiringly.

"I thought you'd never ask," he said, sitting down.

"Can I see Fakwes?"

"How naïve can you get?" He threw up his hands. "The man doesn't say 'Can I see the accused?' — or Mkize, or anything like that. No! He uses some kind of pet nickname! How do you suppose you would sound in court? What does it mean, anyway?"

"Fakwes is short for Ukufakwezwe."

"I see. Does Uku-whatever mean anything?"

"It means 'Death of the Nation.' "

"Christ!" he exclaimed. "Imagine what a prosecutor could make of that in a subversion case! Imagine, the Death of the bloody Nation! 'And which nation were you planning the death of, Mr. Mkize?' "

"Can I see him?" I repeated impatiently.

"I wouldn't advise it," he said seriously. "It would tar you a bit. In case you change your mind, I'd prefer you to stay remote. It would be better for you, too."

"Can I do anything else? Clothes, cigarettes, money? Your fees?"

"Since you ask, since you ask, I'll tell you. I earn my living helping small businessmen who make mistakes. Clients like your friend usually don't have a penny. I handle them *pro deo*. Naturally, I try to avoid incurring expenses. But even so, there's stationery and postage and official fees. And tobacco for the poor bastards. I try to look after things like that, and perhaps get a wife in from the country to see her husband for the last time. It costs. Of course, it's a mitzvah." He assumed a mock Yiddish manner and spread his palms. "You know vot is a mitzvah? A credit up there." He jerked a thumb at the ceiling. "Mitzvahs I got like Job had boils. But can you mit a mitzvah buy a bottle viskey?" He reverted to normal. "You stock an excellent spirit, by the way. Not like some cheapskates, who put away the Black Label and bring out the Japanese when they see me coming."

I refilled his glass and took out my wallet. I like to carry a reasonable amount of cash, and that afternoon I had drawn an extra sum because my wife and I were going to the races the next day. There were always races in Durban on Wednesday afternoons. I took all there was in the wallet and gave it to Benny Miller without counting it.

He weighed it in his palm. "I wish I had a boyhood chum like you," he said. "It's understood that this is an unconditional gift? I use it as I choose, and I don't account for it?"

"I don't know what happened to the money," I replied. "It must have slipped out of my hip pocket in the street when I was tying my shoelace."

He put the money in his pocket. "Okay. But remember

what I've said. Once you've done something like this, things are never quite the same. As the rabbi says, one mitzvah leads to another." He drained his glass and left.

My wife was horrified when I told her what had occurred.

"You've always told me of your wonderful Zulu friend, the David to your Jonathan," she jeered. "And now, when he might be in jail for the rest of his life and you might get a chance to speak for him, you'll think it over. Think it over! I'm ashamed."

"You'd be more than ashamed if the police came and turned the house inside out, looking for God knows what," I retorted.

I kept telling myself that I didn't owe Fakwes that much. I would have owed him if he had been just an ordinary, or even a rather special, black man, like those I met on the Bantu Welfare Committee. With his brains and a bit of help he could have got more education and perhaps become a teacher, or my head clerk, which would pay better. We would have remained friends. He would come to dinner from time to time. My European friends would recognize that they were being given a special treat if they were invited when he and his wife came. But as it was . . . He had nearly killed that youth years ago, and now it seemed he might be a terrorist. Perhaps he was. When he was a boy, he wanted to take the land back from the settlers. Fancy his learning French! I wondered what he looked like. Was he the same person that I had known twenty-five years ago? I was guiltily certain that if I were a fugitive, he would risk his life for me. Or would he? Several kids with whom I had been friendly at school were now only distant acquaintances, whom I might see at Rotary but not otherwise.

At the races the next day my wife ostentatiously put all her money on Bosom Friend at fifty-to-one and won. Someone assured us that Beesknees was a certainty for the main race. I backed him without excitement. Fakwes and I used to rob wild bees' nests. We got up early, because in the cold dawn bees huddle together, more or less inactive. We collected twigs and leaves, made a smoky fire, and blew smoke deep into the nest, which was usually a hole in the ground or in a hollow tree. The smoke stupefied the bees. Fakwes always made me stand some distance away while he chopped and dug to get at the honeycombs. He was often stung. I was occasionally stung too, but I learned not to cry out: one of Fakwes's rules was that one was never allowed to cry for pain. I was always the one who carried the honey home, like a conquering hero, while Fakwes stood by, waving an insect-repellent herb and describing how we had located the nest by following the flight of bees from a flowering tree or by listening to the bee eater. The bee eater has a very pronounced swallowtail and . . .

"Wake up, dreamy Daniel!" My wife shook my elbow. "When you come to the races, you're supposed to care which horse wins." She pointed to the board flashing BEESKNEES 12–1. He had won by three lengths.

The next day I phoned Benny Miller. As soon as he heard my voice he said, "I'll ring back," and put down the receiver. Ten minutes later he called from a pay phone.

"My office phone is tapped," he explained. "What's on your mind?"

"I've decided I will be available as a character witness, or do whatever else you think may help."

"Congratulations. Or perhaps you're psychic. Your friend escaped from custody last night. There is the usual loose talk about venal guards. Anyway, I don't suppose you'll see your pal again unless you rendezvous abroad. Well, so long."

About a month afterwards I received a postcard from Spain. It showed a black bull, its shoulder bristling with lances, kneeling on a bullfighter. That was all. No message, just the wounded black bull triumphing over its adversary. I burned the card. It is not the sort of thing one wants to keep around.

Benny Miller was in the news a couple of times during the next year. A technicality saved him from conviction on a charge of corrupting a customs officer, and he was knocked down the courthouse steps by women protesting against his defense of a black girl who had organized a union of nursemaids.

He called me soon after my return from a visit to Europe. He spoke from a phone booth. "Did you have a good trip? See all the old friends you wanted to see? Look, a fund you know of has developed a deficit like the national debt. Would you care to perpetrate a mitzvah?"

We met in a bar. We did not drink together or greet each other, but he picked up an envelope that I left on the counter.

Eight or nine months later he phoned again, soon after the African bus riots. "Miller here. I'm sure you know why I'm calling."

I hesitated, and he said urgently, "Look, man, the bloody goats are in the field, man."

"Okay," I said. "The Four Seasons bar. Tomorrow at six."

"Bless you," he responded. "Thank God for boyhood chums, eh?"

He phones once or twice every year. He now announces himself as "Benjamin" (that is what his friends call him, he explains) and always asks what news I have from abroad. I always answer "Nothing," but he enjoys teasing me with the suggestion that I am connected with an underground movement. I inquire after his health and may refer to a trial in which he is appearing. Then I mention goats, and he makes a little joke about my accumulation of credits "up there." A good act qualifies as a credit even if it is not entirely voluntary, he says.

The Animal
Lover

JACOBINA VAN TONDER would no more have bought a
book for diversion than bought a man to ease her long-
ings. To read to her small son, Johannes, she therefore
had to rely entirely on the three books that were in the
house — the family Bible; a *Stockman's Veterinary Handbook*, which had come free with a bulk order of Cooper's
sheepdip; and an illustrated copy of Burchell's *List of
Quadrupeds Brought from South Africa and Presented to the
British Museum, 1817.* The Burchell had been part of a
miscellaneous lot that her late husband had bought at an
auction sale for the sake of a carving knife and a painted
lampshade that were also included in it.

The books gave Johannes unfailing pleasure. Long before he went to school he learned to read so that he could
go over his favorite passages without troubling his mother.
He pored over the anatomical pictures in the veterinary
manual, copied them on his slate, and carefully compared
them, first with the carcasses hanging on hooks in the

butchery, and then with the live sheep and oxen on the farm.

In the Bible Johannes liked Noah, Elijah's ravens, and Daniel and the lions. Burchell's *List* was even more exciting, because any walk on the farm was likely to yield a sighting of a hare or other small creature, which suggested that if one went into the thicker, forbidden bush there might be bigger animals — sable antelope, koodoo, wildebeest, quagga — gazing into the distance with that calm, farsighted look they always had in the illustrations.

He earned good marks at school. He was, however, not a popular boy. His collections of live and dead creatures, and his frank interest in all their bodily functions, including mating and parturition, were a constant source of embarrassment to teachers. Even worse were his distorted values about how people should behave towards animals, typified by his reaction to the story of Paul Kruger's thumb. Hunting alone in the bushveld, the story goes, Paul Kruger encountered a lion, which bit him on the thumb. Knowing that a lion bite often causes fatal blood poisoning, he cut off his thumb with his hunting knife and cauterized the wound by setting gunpowder alight on it. He thereby saved his own life and went on to become president of the South African Republic and to lead his people in their struggle against British domination. Johannes was unimpressed: he argued passionately that if Paul Kruger had been kinder to lions, like, say, Androcles, his gruesome bravery would have been unnecessary.

At the university it took some argument before Johannes was allowed to major in biology and divinity, but his palpable sincerity won the day, and he was allowed to read his improbable combination of subjects. After graduating he joined the civil service, where he rose at the rate his unbrilliant steadiness, honesty, and hard work merited. He lived frugally, saving all he could. As soon as he had enough for the deposit, he bought a small farm just out of town. For the sake of appearances, he kept a few cows and chickens, but the main purpose of the farm was to provide a home for all the tame, half-tame, healthy, or unhealthy antelope and other wild creatures he could lay hands on. He accepted all that were brought to him, nursed the sick, sedated the dying, and coaxed the celibate in mating.

He had no friends, but was well regarded by fellow members of the Zoological Society and of the Safari Club. He avoided women, went to church regularly — the Dutch Reformed Church — and spent his holidays either tending the creatures on his farm or visiting research stations and wildlife refuges.

His mother died when he was fifty, leaving him a surprising amount of money. He knew exactly what to do with it. Up near the border, twenty miles from a small village, was a ranch of some eight thousand acres, virtually abandoned by its owner, who had been almost bankrupted by trying to run cattle in an area so full of game. All efforts to free cattle from ticks were frustrated by reinfestations from antelope; tsetse flies spread nagana, a disease that killed cattle but did not affect wild animals; and despite shooting, poisoning, and trapping, lions, hyenas, cheetahs, and leopards abounded, all apparently finding domestic cattle to be tastier and easier prey than antelope, zebras, and warthogs.

Johannes drove from his mother's funeral through the

night, made an offer for the ranch, and received an ac-
ceptance by noon the next day. He returned, sent in his
resignation to his department head, and put his farm on
the market, all in one afternoon.

Two months later he was settling in on his ranch, un-
packing crates of veterinary appliances and medicines and
the books he had acquired. Most of the books were concerned with zoology, but he had also bought several dozen
Greek and Roman classics in translation, a few theological
works, and a range of Dutch and Flemish authors — in
fact, all the books he had always thought he would like
to read if he had time.

Life on his ranch turned out to be all that he had hoped
for. He had leisure, was surrounded by wildlife, and had
enough to live on: his small investment income was enough
to pay for his truck, wages for a couple of servants, food,
clothes, and animal medicines. Though he sowed no crops
for harvest, he planted patches of beans, pumpkins, sweet
potatoes, and birdseed at points he could watch from his
living room or from a lookout on his roof. The distinctive
green patches attracted all kinds of creatures. A solitary
eland took possession of the derelict orchard, eating sour
oranges with an evident mixture of desire and distaste,
and sneezing comically in response to the pungent oils.
A zebra mare with a damaged leg found sanctuary under
a verandah and foaled there. A little wild pig that had
begun by picking scraps of bread and porridge from the
rubbish heap was soon imperiously butting at the kitchen
door if his meal was late. Doves of several varieties com-
peted for the scraps, and partridges and guinea fowl were
soon to be seen openly feeding near the house, watched
almost as openly by a jackal.

Over a period of months Johannes tried out a dozen or so native servants and finally settled on two who appeared to have a genuine feeling for wild creatures. Both of them had at one time hunted for a living, and were as comfortable in the bush as they were at home. They taught Johannes a great deal of practical bushcraft. In turn, he tried to tell them something about animal physiology and about animal life in other parts of the world. They listened with grave attention, and only afterwards, in private, did they give way to their laughter at such fairy-tale creatures as bucks whose horns grew in branches and fell off every year, leaping animals that carried their young in pouches, and hares that turned white in the winter.

Their relationship with Johannes gradually ripened, not quite into friendship, but certainly into a sense of common purpose. When talking to each other, they had originally called Johannes "Fat Bum"; they now saluted him with upraised hands as "Silent One, Herdsman of the Cattle of God." Ignorant of their language, Johannes took the greeting to be no more than an elaborate African version of good morning. He had no interest in what they thought, except in relation to animals — indeed, he did not even recall their names, but habitually addressed them as Jim One and Jim Two.

Apart from acquaintances whom he occasionally invited for a day's shooting, he had few relationships with the rest of the community. When he visited the village store or the post office, he chatted courteously about the weather, crops, and unfavorable foreign news, but did not linger once he had done his business. He paid cash for what he bought, never borrowed, had nothing to lend, and declined all invitations.

The one exception to his solitude was the church. He attended regularly, dignified and black-clad, and in due course became an elder. His education, gravity, dispassionate attitude, and appropriate contributions to church funds earned him a respect only slightly diminished by the amazement and suspicion that his eccentricity engendered. It seemed to some that owning eight thousand acres and doing nothing with them, not even selling game for meat, was either sinful or was at least so unproductive that it should be prohibited by law. There were also those who wondered how and why a healthy and personable man could remain single. It was, they argued, almost a man's Christian duty to take care of one of the many widows in the district. Before he was made an elder, some senior elders, together with the local police sergeant, investigated the position with great thoroughness, even offering substantial bribes to one of Johannes's servants; but they uncovered no black concubine nor any surreptitious visits to Johannesburg or anywhere else.

In course of time men of his own age, or older, ceased to call him Mr. van Tonder, first addressing him as Johannes, and finally slipping into the familiar John or Hannes. Behind his back he was referred to as John Game Park.

The first year of the drought was treated by all as one of those things that happen, but against the effects of which the prudent had guarded by creating reserve stocks of hay and other feed, and by keeping their mortgages low. The second year was hard even for the prudent, and devastating for the thriftless and poor. Worst hit were the

Africans. They had neither subsistence crops nor means of earning cash, for employment on the farms and in the villages had virtually ceased. There were reports of famine deaths and rumors of infanticides.

It was only to be expected that starving people should turn more readily to the meat that was accessible on Johannes's ranch. He had put up windmills at several of the waterholes, and here one could almost walk among the herds of zebras and antelope.

Johannes knew that African poaching was on the increase, but was not greatly concerned. He regarded an occasional poacher as just another predator playing its part in maintaining ecological balance. He and his two servants patrolled the ranch regularly, and the poachers kept out of their way, as if by mutual understanding. As a precaution, he took to shooting a few hyenas and cheetahs every week, on the principle that their removal would counterbalance the increase in human predation.

His tolerance ceased the day he found the bushbuck. It was not dead but nearly so, with the steel-wire noose cutting deep into its throat. It had obviously been snared some days earlier; the hunter had simply not visited his trap. Over the next week or two Johannes found other such animals. Some had broken the noose or torn out the peg. All had endured days of dreadful suffering. Moreover, it appeared from these cases, as from the bushbuck, that the snarer set nooses but often failed to come back for his prizes.

The inept hunter's work was distinctive, and Johannes was soon able to find where his other snares were. He undid each noose he found, leaving it dangling conspicuously, as if an animal had tripped the trigger and escaped. He worked out where a man would have to stand to reach the noose and pull it down to reset it. At each of these points he dug a shallow pit, carefully keeping the turf in one piece. In the pits he placed lion traps — massive iron things with great teeth — that the former owner of the ranch had left behind. He carefully replaced the sod on top of the traps and carried away soil from the pits so that his work should not be readily detected.

He visited his man traps each afternoon. On the fourth day he found a catch — a miserable little man, gray with pain, fright, and loss of blood. Johannes tied his hands behind his back, released his leg, and dragged him to a nearby tree. Jim One, who was patrolling close by, came forward to help, but Johannes waved him away. He lashed the man to the tree and tied his head back and his chin down to keep his mouth open. Then with a pair of fencing pliers from his pouch he systematically extracted or broke off the poacher's teeth, all except three, which he possibly overlooked in the welter of blood. Finally he released the battered, fainting man. Only then did he notice that the African had a withered, useless right arm.

The poacher dragged himself home. His relatives wheeled him twenty miles in a wheelbarrow to the hospital, and the doctors called the police. Johannes did not deny the facts, but pleaded not guilty to the assault charge. He seemed to find it hard to understand the court's horror; it was so clear to him that anyone who tortured animals should be repaid in kind. He paid the large fine with a sense of injustice.

Jim One gave evidence at the trial. He testified that he

had assisted in setting the man traps and had witnessed Johannes's capture of the poacher. He had thought Johannes was performing some kind of ritual to appease the spirits of animals that had died in an unacceptable way.

The white community's response to the affair was muddled by revelations about the poacher. It turned out that he had some months before been the victim of a hit-and-run accident. His twisted right arm was one consequence; another was some mental incapacity, reflected in, among other things, chronic forgetfulness. He had never brought home any of the meat he snared. He had five children and a tuberculous wife. Ladies of the church auxiliary indignantly urged the authorities to do something about the family. Several farmers, more practically minded, sent gifts of corn, meal, pumpkins, and tallow. The storekeeper, who was widely suspected of being the hit-and-run driver, contributed a large carton of groceries, many of which were still usable. The police decided not to prosecute the man for illegal hunting, since they could not connect him directly with any individual animal.

When Johannes arrived at church the Sunday after the trial, some worshippers moved away so as not to sit next to him. At the communion service the following Sunday he again found himself sitting alone. When the pitcher of sacramental wine was passed from hand to hand, the last man in the pew ahead of him ignored Johannes's outstretched fingers and passed the wine across to a man in the pew behind him; there were subdued nods of approval. After the service the minister, accompanied by two elders, told him he was no longer acceptable as an elder. Congregational censure was proposed but was not pursued, because some farmers contended that Johannes's offense lay essentially in his having a wrong reason for what he had done. If the poacher had, say, maimed cattle instead of game, Johannes might have been justified. It seemed to them that Johannes was just as confused as the poacher was.

Throughout his life Johannes had shunned people without ever feeling lonely. Now, when people shunned him, his isolation sometimes became unbearable, and then he drove to the village's little hotel to spend the evening austerely drinking coffee and an occasional brandy. He spoke no more, but also no less, than before, and showed no emotion when he learned that his nickname was now John Dentist.

Tom and Beauty

◈

WE DIDN'T HAVE VIDEOS and peace movements in those days, so what we talked about were things like who made God, and should you tell your father if your mother was cheating on him.

Arabelle Jones's mother cheated when she went to dances, but Arabelle didn't tell her father: it would just make him more downtrodden. He was such a milktoast, he wouldn't do anything except perhaps desert her and her mother, and Arabelle would miss him. Mr. Jones was rich.

Tom and Della Barton's mother cheated every Thursday night; Mr. Barton went off to his mine Sunday afternoon and came back Friday night. She cheated with Mr. Percival, who kept the store where we bought our candies. Mr. Percival knew that Tom and Della knew. We often noticed him looking very hard at them, and they got about twice as much for a penny as anyone else. He never gave them anything free, though he sometimes smiled in a skew way, showing overcrowded teeth on one side of his mouth. We looked up to Mr. Percival, because he was a famous marksman. One year he was runner-up in the national .22 championship.

Tom and Della didn't tell Mr. Barton because they didn't like him. My friend Ed and I liked our fathers, but a lot of kids didn't much like theirs. They boasted about them, though, like how strong they were or how much they drank. Ed boasted that his father shot game out of season and had secret routes for bringing in the meat: he sometimes sent joints of venison to the police constable and to the parson. The joints were always beautifully larded with thin strips of bacon fat. Ed and I used to take the joint around to Constable Plough's kitchen, leave it on the doorstep, then retire behind the fence and throw stones at the door until someone opened it and found the joint before a dog got it. We wondered who Constable Plough thought the meat came from.

Tom and Della boasted how fierce their pa was. He didn't look fierce except for his mustache, which had sharp shiny points. When you greeted him he twirled one mustache point and said, "Hello there, kid, did your goat eat Granny's britches?"

Della went everywhere with Tom. He wouldn't come to play unless she was asked, too, and he always made sure she was picked for a team and had her chance to bat, and things like that. He called her "sweetie," even at school. She was very pretty, with round green eyes just like Mr. Barton's. Because I didn't have a mother she always treated me as though I needed comforting. I remember liking it.

We knew Mr. Barton really was fierce, because once
when someone suggested we go swimming in the old
brick field Della said no, she and Tommy were not going.
Ed teased, "Aw, Della, come on. We won't look at your
titties." She had begun to be shy about swimming without her swimsuit top, so I said, "Well, Tom can swim.
You can sit on the chimney and watch for enemies. Pretend you are See Far Woman." We didn't play Indians
anymore, so this was putting her down a bit. "Come on,
Tom."

Della held Tom's arm. "Don't go, Tommy, don't let
them see, Tommy. There'll be trouble, Tommy."

Tom patted her. "Don't you worry, sweetie, nobody
will tell. Hey, you guys, promise you won't tell if I show
you a big thing?"

We all said, "Scout's honor," and crowded round,
thinking he must have had himself tattooed or something.

He peeled off his shirt. His back was crossed with wide
red weals from being belted. His pa had thrashed him
with a belt because he hadn't done his chores properly.
You could see places where the buckle had hit, breaking
the skin in a square. Della wouldn't let us touch the weals,
because we might be rough. She put lard on the marks
every night when they went to bed.

Tom's main chores were looking after Mr. Barton's
mare, Beauty. She was a fifteen-hand bay with a very
beautiful blaze; Mr. Barton let everyone know that she
was half thoroughbred. Tom had to clean out her stable
every morning, groom her with a curry comb and a
brush, and finish off with a yellow duster that had been

sprinkled with a teaspoon of coal oil; then he took her
out to the common lands before school. He always smelled
a little of coal oil and horse, and the insides of his legs
were quite hairless from his bareback riding.

Every day just before sunset he had to fetch Beauty
and stable and feed her, and so he couldn't be on any of
the school teams.

The chore he'd been thrashed for was the Baber fly
trap. It was a cage of wire netting for storing manure.
Mr. Barton knew about it from his British army days.
Flies laid eggs in the manure, and by the time the maggots
hatched, the manure had heated up so much they fled to
the outside of the cage and fell through the netting into
a tray below. You were supposed to have carbolic or coal
oil in the tray to kill the maggots, but Tom put down
sawdust instead so that he could collect the maggots and
sell them to anglers and bird fanciers. The Barton kids
didn't get allowances like the rest of us or get paid for
working around the yard, so maggot raising was
Tom's way of making money. One Friday he forgot to
clean out the trays, and Saturday morning there were
dozens of crawling little white worms for Mr. Barton
to see.

Weekends, Mr. Barton rode Beauty out into the country for hunts or races. He wore jodhpurs that made his
legs look very thin, a silk shirt, and a neckcloth that he
called an Ascot. He rode with a short stirrup, British style.
He liked people to think he was a remittance man, but
the postmaster said the checks he got from England were
a disability pension from being a corporal in some mule
transport outfit. Beauty usually came back steaming and

lathered from Mr. Barton's weekend gallops. Then Tom walked her till she was cool, rubbed her down with sacking and straw, and brushed her till she shone again.

Whenever he went past her Tom would spit, "Goddam bloody horse." He spent a lot of time in the library reading about horse diseases and plants that are poisonous to horses. We helped him collect yew berries, ragwort seeds, and sweet pea seeds, because the veterinary books warned against them. Tom put them into Beauty's feed and waited for her to develop staggers from the ragwort, or something called lathyritic paralysis from the sweet peas, but nothing ever happened. I forget what the yew berries were supposed to do. The books said moldy peanuts were another good poison; we found half a sackful behind the store and gave them to Tom. Beauty wouldn't touch them.

Beauty had one big weakness: she was terrified of lightning. If she was caught in a storm, she would rear and plunge about without looking where she was going. Once she threw Mr. Barton. Another time she ran right into a barbed wire fence and cut herself all round the chest and neck. To protect her during storms, she had to be blindfolded with big blinkers or by a special leather bag pulled tightly over her head, with a hole for her nostrils. Sometimes Tom even took off from school to blinker Beauty if a storm was brewing.

One hot afternoon Tom and Della and I and some of the other kids were at Ed's place. We had just learned to play poker and were gambling with all the money we had. Tom won almost every game. He wasn't usually the best at anything except target shooting, so he really enjoyed the way his pile of pennies grew. He concentrated so hard he seemed not to notice the flashes of lightning and crashes of thunder from a storm that was blowing up. Della kept on telling him the storm was getting worse and Beauty would panic and hurt herself. She appealed to us: "Pa said if anything bad happened to Beauty, he'd do the same thing to Tommy. He will, too. That time when Beauty ran into the fence he took a piece of barbed wire to Tommy. Oh, please stop him!"

We said, "Hey, Tom, what about that horse, eh?" But he went on playing and winning. He kept pulling his mouth skew and showing his deformed teeth on one side, like Mr. Percival, and muttering things like "I hope that goddam mare will shit her guts out in terror" and "My goddam pa will never know because he'll only be home goddam Friday night." Della cried, pulling at him and pleading, "Please, Tommy, please." She tried to take his cards away. He didn't take his eyes off his cards, just put his left arm round her and held her tight. "Quiet, sweetie. Sit still and bring your Tommy luck. You'll see, it'll be lucky for you too."

Eventually Ed's mother came and stopped the game because it was near suppertime. Tom seemed suddenly to wake up and realize where he was. There was a thunder clap and a big flash of lightning. "Oh, goddam," he cursed, "that goddam horse will hurt herself and Pa will lather me. He'll lather the hide off me. If that mare has broken her leg, he'll break my goddam leg. Oh, Jesus, please Jesus, don't let that mare be hurt." He ran out into the storm without even a jacket. He was crying, he was so frightened.

When the rain stopped, Della and the rest of us went home. Della wanted me to go out with her to look for Tom: if anything had happened to Beauty she thought Tom might run away because he'd be so scared of what their pa might do. He sometimes imagined things that were much worse than what Mr. Barton actually did. Once when he had done something wrong and was waiting for Mr. Barton to come on Friday, he didn't eat for two days. He crapped all over his bedroom floor and rolled in it and didn't hear anything anyone said. I said no, Tom would feel bad about us coming out to look for him; he could look after himself.

I kept an eye on the common lands road, expecting to see Tom come back riding Beauty. When he had not yet returned by sunset I phoned Mrs. Barton, but there was no reply. Father eventually phoned the police. Constable Plough said the matter was under investigation and they would be grateful for any light we could cast on it; he would be along shortly. He wouldn't say over the phone what he was talking about.

When he arrived, he and Father had a whispered conversation; then Father came and put his arm round me, as if I were a little boy, and said, "Mr. Plough has a sad thing to tell you, and he wants to ask you some questions."

Constable Plough was careful, but it was clear enough: Tom had been found hanged from the high crossbar of the gate to the common lands. Old Mrs. Wentzel, whose house overlooked the road, saw him climb up the gate. She was thinking how naughty it was when he seemed to fall, dangling and kicking. By the time Mr. Wentzel got there with his stepladder, Tom was not kicking any-more. Mr. Wentzel was rather slow on account of his arthritis.

It didn't look like an accident, Mr. Plough thought; the rope had been tied firmly to the crossbar, and the noose was also made with a neat knot. He wanted to know about Tom's afternoon. I told him about our card game, and Tom winning, and the storm, which of course he knew about. He was shocked when I asked where Beauty was. "Your best friend dead and you want to know about a horse!" Tom wasn't my best friend, he wasn't anybody's best friend, but it didn't matter.

"Well, young fellow, the horse was up to her neck in a mud pool. Damned if I know how she got in there. Your friend tried to dig her out with his hands; half his fingernails were torn off. Now, if he had just been able to push something under her forefeet; if a horse can just get its forefeet onto something solid, it can pull itself out, you know. With a cow, it's just the opposite. Ever notice when a cow is lying down and gets up, it starts with the back legs? And a horse always with its front legs? Once we'd freed her front legs, out she came." He turned to my father. "I reckon that poor boy loved that horse too much. When he thought she was done for, sinking to death in the mud, he couldn't bear it. Must be a dreadful death, feeling the mud creep up to your mouth. And then to your nostrils . . ."

"Yeah," Father said. "How's your drink?"

Mr. Plough went on. "Like a slow torture. I think savages put their enemies into quicksands in Africa, don't they?"

"Another storm brewing," Father said, trying to protect me from the scary picture Mr. Plough was painting.
He need not have been so concerned: I wasn't thinking
about the mud; I was imagining Tom kicking on the rope.
Was he dead as soon as the rope jerked, or did he feel the
noose tightening and try to pull himself up and free himself? Maybe that was why his fingernails were broken. If
it was me, I would use a long rope so that the drop would
be sure to break my neck immediately. It has to snap the
spinal cord, I had heard. But you had to be careful not
to make the drop too long; otherwise the rope might
break.

Suppose I had gone out looking for Tom when Della
wanted us to? And suppose I had got there just after he
had jumped, when he was still trying to tear the rope
loose? I saw myself climbing up the gate. I couldn't get
up on the crossbar fast enough. When I did reach it I
couldn't cut the rope, because my knife sheath had a
broken strap that had let it slip off my belt. The knife
and sheath lay on the ground below, and I had to climb
down and fetch them and climb back again. Meantime
Tom was making a funny noise . . .

Father poured a shot of brandy into a glass of ginger
ale and gave it to me. "Here, take this, my boy," he said.
"You need it as much as we do." I had never had brandy
before except in a hot toddy to bring out the spots when
I had measles. Though I didn't like the taste, I drank it
slowly, because it was an event and because I had wanted
to ask Mr. Plough a lot of questions. However, Father
had got him arguing about storms and barometric pres-
sures, and I fell asleep.

The minister hurried the police surgeon to get the post mortem done so that Tom's funeral would not be delayed. Father thought the minister wanted it over and done with before some church member raised questions about suicides and potter's fields. I hadn't known till then that suicide was a sin.

The whole school went to the funeral. At other funerals I had been to, people filed past the family and shook each person's hand or touched their shoulders. Some people shook Mrs. Barton's hand, but not Mr. Barton's. Della went and stood by Mr. Percival. She and Mr. Percival were the only people who cried; that is, until the eulogy, which was spoken by Tom's teacher. The teacher kept turning and waving one arm as if he were disappointed that there wasn't a blackboard. He related how Tom had been pretty smart and attentive, though sometimes he excused himself to go to the bathroom, when in fact he had gone off to see if Beauty was all right; nearly all the books Tom read were about horses; one time when the class went for a weekend to the mountains Tom didn't go because he didn't want to leave Beauty unattended. By the time the teacher finished, a number of people were crying. I heard afterwards some pony breeders were angry, because they feared parents would be worried about their kids getting too attached to horses.

After the service Della didn't go with her parents; instead, she came with me and we walked part of the way with Mr. Percival. He was still pretty upset, but when we parted, he smiled his skew smile and said, "You were a kind friend to Tom. Thank you," and shook my hand.

TOM AND BEAUTY

Hardly anybody went to the Bartons' for the funeral lunch except the women from the church guild who had made the food, and a few of Mr. Barton's riding friends. Della and I stayed in the garden. She kept on saying Tommy must have done the right thing: she was sure her pa would have thrown Tommy in the mud pool. She thought she could have fed Tom for a while with food on a stick and given him water on a sponge like they did for Jesus, but what would she have done when the mud reached his face? I said we would have rescued him long before that, using old doors and the inner tubes we had at the brick field.

One of the church ladies came looking for Della, and I went on home. About five o'clock Constable Plough came by in a great hurry, calling out for Father. Father took his twelvebore and they accelerated down the drive like madmen. All I got was that Mr. Barton had killed Mrs. Barton and wounded Della and a church lady who had stayed to help sort out dishes and cutlery.

The hospital said Della was okay; she only had a couple of shotgun pellets in her legs. She was under sedation and they were sure I would be able to see her tomorrow.

Father and Constable Plough returned late that night. I suddenly realized what my father would look like when he was old — pale and thin, and with deep lines down his cheeks. He and Mr. Plough each swallowed a double brandy in one gulp and then went on to beers. I watched their faces both plumping up, like when a raisin swells in water.

I couldn't get much out of Father, but Constable Plough told me all about it. I think he was getting things straight

in his mind for his report. Apparently the lady who was
wounded escaped to the nearest neighbor. Pretty soon
her husband got together ten or fifteen men and several
women. They went out with Dobermans and guns, looking for Mr. Barton. No one called the police — possibly
everyone thought someone else had done so. As a result
Constable Plough first heard of it from the ambulance
driver. He rushed to get Father because Father was the
nearest solid citizen he could think of who wouldn't be
out with the rest.

They found the mob at the common lands gate ready
to hang Mr. Barton. His hands were tied behind his back,
and he was standing on the back of a truck parked under
the gate. A rope with a noose at one end was tied to the
crossbar, ready for putting round his neck. The idea was
then to drive the truck away, though afterwards they all
said they wouldn't actually have done it.

Mr. Percival and a couple of women were trying to
stop the hanging. When Father and Constable Plough
appeared, Mr. Percival gave a big shout, "Look at that,
fellows!" and pointed to Beauty, who was grazing fifty
yards or so beyond the gate. Then he shot her.

"He shot Beauty?"

"Right between the eyes," Mr. Plough said. You could
tell he admired the marksmanship. "She dropped and
screamed — nasty sound, a wounded horse's scream. The
mob crowded round her, and two or three fellows each
put a shot into her; at least that's what it sounded like —
I was too busy to look. Your father pushed Barton flat
onto the truckbed and I got into the cab and drove away
before they knew what we were doing."

TOM AND BEAUTY

Ed and I went out to look at Beauty's carcass next day. She was swollen to double normal size, and bluebottles were crawling up her nostrils and buzzing round under her tail. She didn't look polished anymore. I kicked the carcass a couple of times, and Ed and I both said, "Poor old Tom, eh."

Spirits Do Not Forgive

AT MITCHELL'S LIQUID PACKAGING some employees were
called "the girls" and some "the boys." "The girls" com-
prised Annie, the middle-aged secretary, and Shirley, the
bookkeeper, who were white, and Bonnie, the black cash-
ier and statistics clerk. "The boys" were the black laborers
in the yard.

Vilakazi, the foreman, was black, but he certainly was
not a "boy." He was called "Mr. Vilakazi" or "Mr. V."
The laborers had all been engaged by him, and all were
members of his clan. Some were paid a few cents an hour
more than others because they were important in the
clan's hierarchy. Three or four times in his twenty years
at Mitchell's, Vilakazi had sacked a man, but otherwise
the same individuals played a kind of musical chairs, two
or three at a time going home to Kwa Zulu and being
replaced by others. They were not paid during their ab-
sences, which might last three or four months — longer
if a wife was tardy to conceive or if ceremonies had to

be performed for a relative's death — but Vilakazi kept them on the books so that there would be no trouble about influx control or work permits when they returned.

Vilakazi did not spend his own holidays in Zululand. Instead, he visited Johannesburg, Pretoria, or Cape Town "just to look." He could afford to travel, because he was paid almost as much as a white foreman would have been. He came to work in a big blue 1960 Buick that he and the native mechanic had salvaged from a motor graveyard and fitted with a new engine, also from a graveyard. The Buick's size, spotless paintwork, and white-wall tires gave it an old-fashioned millionaire-ish look. Once, when Mr. Mitchell's car broke down the day before he had to leave for Johannesburg, Vilakazi offered his, and Mr. Mitchell accepted. He said afterwards he got the Oxenham contract because Oxenham's British executives were so impressed by his enormous, almost-vintage car.

Annie and Shirley had joined Mitchell's soon after Vilakazi, and felt a respect and affection for him that they found hard to describe. "He's not exactly a colleague," Shirley explained to her sister, "and he's not a friend, because, well, it's not as if I would invite him to dinner or kiss him for Merry Christmas, you know, but if I asked him to lend me his whole month's salary, he wouldn't even ask for how long, and if he died we'd be as sad as if he was, you know, one of us. And he's very good-looking, for a Bantu." Vilakazi was tall and lean and straight. He had magnificent short white teeth and beautiful manners, learned at the mission boarding school he had attended.

Bonnie often made it clear that she was after Vilakazi.

"Anything he wants from me he can have. I'll give him anything. Anything," she often declared.

When she did so, Annie would twit her, "Haven't you given it away already, dear?" Bonnie had two children and a succession of boyfriends.

Vilakazi teased Bonnie gently, greeting her with archaic native praise-names, always ending with "She-elephant! You thunder even when sitting down." Bonnie said these were the titles of a Zulu or Swazi queen, and not a reference to her own plumpness. "In any case, Bantu men do not like skinny girls," she said.

"But haven't you outgrown these tribal customs?" Annie persisted. "With your education . . ."

"I am not speaking of tri*bal*. These things are tradi-tio*nal*, not tri*bal*. You do not call a Christmas tree tri*bal*." She was very keen on African cultures and had done two years of social anthropology before she got pregnant and lost her bursary. "Just because these Boer bastards want to disintegrate us into many little tribes does not mean we must throw away our culture. We are not just Zulu and Sotho and Venda. We are Azanian; all the tribes are Azanian. You should read psych and anthro. Then you will understand. You see, you whities have an uncon-scious full of sex, like Freud. We Azanians do not have sex guilt, man. We have a racial unconscious, like Jung. Black consciousness comes from race memory. I feel it here," she said, poking a finger at her navel. "I am not tri*bal*. Those whores are tri*bal*."

She was referring to the native women who lounged all day under the jacaranda trees at the intersection where a path led from the industrial area to the single men's hostels. The women wore squares of dark red fabric or off-white "kaffir sheeting," knotted together over one shoulder and fastened under the other armpit with a safety pin, leaving one breast exposed unless the garment was deliberately hitched up. The massive bead belts that curved over their fat round bellies pulled the cloth squares in, to reveal great expanses of oiled skin. It came as a surprise to Annie and Shirley that these women were not country innocents decked in their finery to visit their husbands or sweethearts.

There was nothing tribal or traditional about Vilakazi except his iziqu. He wore two thin, flat pieces of wood, a couple of inches long, on a leather thong round his neck. They had crisscross knife marks on them but were not decorative. No one would have dared ask Vilakazi about them, any more than about any other aspect of his private life, but Bonnie told the other girls: "It is very old and traditional. They are charms to ward off evil that might be done to you by the spirit of a man you have killed. In the old days a great warrior might have a whole necklace of them. I have never seen any except Mr. V's, but I know it from my anthro, and what my grandpa told me. It is very black traditional."

"Oh, I see. Like scalps, or notches on a cowboy's gun," Shirley said.

"No! They are not like that!" Bonnie corrected her indignantly. "They are not for boasting. They are for repelling the ghost of a person you have killed. They are for saying to the spirit of that person, 'I fear you. Keep away from me, please.'"

"Who did Mr. V kill, then? He's not a killing type, is

he?" They were shaken by the thought that someone they had known for years, and trusted, could be a killer — and of two people, because he wore two of the wooden charms. It was with great relief that they recalled the accident years ago when a drunk biker, with a pillion rider, had crashed into the truck Vilakazi was driving.

The Oxenham contract involved so much more business that Mr. Mitchell brought in a junior partner and another girl. The girl was Maxine, a pretty blonde. Vilakazi and his iziqu fascinated her.

"How do you know they are for the men on that motorbike?" she asked. "He wouldn't need to worry about their spirits. It was their fault. Those death charms must be for men he killed in a fight or something." She shuddered pleasurably.

She arranged her chair so that when Vilakazi came in from the yard he would see her crossed legs and her breasts in outline. She made sure that her skirt rode up on that side; then, when Vilakazi came in, she pulled at it, drawing attention to her legs and possibly showing a glimpse of panty in the process.

Annie and Shirley were shocked. "It's not nice, dearie, flaunting yourself before a man. And he's a Bantu, my girl. What will you do if he believes you and creeps up behind you one day in that blue Buick of his?"

Bonnie laughed at her tricks. "You will not catch a hawk with chickenfeed," she said. It was never clear when she was quoting ancient black wisdom and when she was inventing it.

The junior partner was Patrick Brink. As befitted his

degree in industrial management, he was very thorough. He went through the books like an auditor, studying inventories, throughputs, production flows, and labor costs, and covered the walls of his small office with graphs in various colors. He had done well in a management program "Human Relations in the Office," and set about putting it into effect. "If I call you Shirley and Annie, you call me Patrick. Fair's fair, eh?" He was not sure what to do about Bonnie — his program had not dealt with black office staff — and so he did not specifically include her in the invitation. She retaliated by making a habit of going into his office with a sheet of statistics whenever his girlfriend came to pick him up from work. Bonnie would then fetch his jacket, brush off imaginary lint, and comment to the girlfriend on his health and appearance, as if she and the girlfriend shared an interest in him. "She'll think he thinks black is beautiful," she said, chuckling. "It is, too."

"I'd like to go through the yard operations on a work-study basis. Time and motion, you know," Patrick proposed to Mr. Mitchell.

"Go ahead," Mr. Mitchell said. "I'll tell Mr. V. You couldn't have a better instructor."

In the go-down Patrick discovered three drums of paint that had been there for six years, a small colony of bats, and an unopened parcel of pump parts about which Annie had been conducting an acrimonious correspondence with the suppliers. He called Vilakazi in to his office and sternly recounted his finds. He did not ask Vilakazi to sit down, but Vilakazi pushed the "In" tray aside, perched on the corner of Patrick's desk, and thanked him. "It's a help to have a clever expert going through the place, Patrick man. We get so we don't see what's in front of us."

Mr. Mitchell was unsurprised by Patrick's discoveries in the go-down, especially the pump parts, which he now remembered he had tucked on top of a high shelf. He appeared to think that the inspection revealed nothing except how clever it was of Mitchell's Packaging to have found and kept Vilakazi. "Best foreman in Industriville," he declared. "Paulsens and Rembrandt would give their ears for him, but he suits us and we suit him."

Patrick was disappointed but proceeded with his work-study. Stopwatch in hand, he recorded how long it took to move a drum to the filling point, how long filling took, how long it took to fit the bung, how long to move and stack the filled container. He knew from previous experience that foremen were usually difficult about efficiency studies. Vilakazi, however, was fascinated by the stopwatch and by the squares, circles, arrows, and other symbols on Patrick's flow chart. "It's like Boy Scout code," he said with delight. "I was leader of the Bear Patrol at the mission station."

Patrick had abandoned his study, without having any suggestions to offer, when Vilakazi burst into his office one morning, waving a sheet of squared paper on which he had redesigned the layout. He attributed the scheme entirely to Patrick. "You are clever, Patrick. If we do like you say, you see, if we start here, this side of the shed, we can get all drums moving through by their own weight, and we won't waste power lifting them.

"Continuous gravity flow," he added, parroting Patrick's phrase like a magical incantation.

Patrick followed his exposition with interest. "Hey, that's a real professional job."

Vilakazi looked down modestly. "In Zululand they say even a drunkard can cross a swamp once the pathfinder has shown the way."

"That's neat," Patrick said. "Ancient wisdom is kind of pithy, isn't it?"

The troubles began in August, but long before that the streets quite suddenly seemed to have fewer African women on them. The bead- and basket-sellers in the beach areas thinned out; the visiting wives' quarters of men's hostels unexpectedly had vacancies instead of three-month waiting lists; only the hardiest prostitutes kept their stations under the jacaranda trees. Post offices experienced a surge of demand for money orders from migrant laborers sending home the cash they had been saving. Companies with safe custody facilities for employees found their safes bulging. Shebeen keepers stocked up. Bored young men in the townships made sure they would be able to lay their hands on weapons when the time came. They did not know what the violence would be about; it was enough to know that there would be violence: violence, excitement, and the exaltation of being top dog, if only for a day.

Lower-level white officials who saw what was happening nodded wisely over their Castle lagers. "Black kids and migrants expecting trouble," they told one another. "Expecting it or planning it. Remember 'forty-nine?" No one told the authorities, or if they did, it was written off as no more than a little hiccup in the chronic unrest.

Vilakazi did not say anything about trouble brewing, but he diverted the mechanic and half a dozen laborers to check and strengthen the corrugated-iron perimeter fence and its barbed wire canopy, and moved everything that was inflammable away from the perimeter. "Tidying the place," he said apologetically.

When the second black policeman's home was set alight, radio and newspaper reporters did not even hear of it, but Vilakazi told Mr. Mitchell, and asked whether he could leave his car in the yard for a while: it looked too much as if it might belong to a white person or to a rich black collaborator. He would probably have to miss work for a few days: if so, the native mechanic could run the yard. He, Vilakazi, had nominated four very trustworthy, sober laborers to serve as extra night watchmen, and had talked to the foremen on adjoining factories about sharing guards and warnings. Mr. Mitchell did not ask why Vilakazi would have to be away, but watched anxiously as the boys covered the Buick with old black tarpaulins.

That night the riots started in earnest. Mobs of dock laborers swept up from the harbor and circled in thundering waves round the verges of the business district before settling down on the wharves to roast looted meat. In the African townships children attacked liquor stores, offices, schools, taxis, police vans, ambulances, and the homes of township officials. Patrick was called up for emergency military duty. A lot of Mitchell's work was for the army, and Mr. Mitchell thought he might get Patrick exempted, but Patrick said, "No, a man has to do his duty. Like my dad used to say in his war, No he-man is a key-man, eh?"

Next day Bonnie was also absent, to nobody's surprise, for buses had stopped running on several routes.

The troubles flared, subsided, flared again, breaking out in unexpected places, like veld fires sparked by erratic winds and dust devils. After a week they died down, not indeed into peace, but into a kind of ashen blanket under which patches of embers still smoldered. "Till next time!" tired gangs of rioters shouted to one another as they returned to their shanties. "Amandla!"

Patrick was back within ten days. He was uncommunicative about his experiences except to agree that his unit had been on duty at Muzimuhle township, and to say repeatedly that mob control was not proper work for soldiers. Annie related that her nephew felt the same. He had seen their jobbing gardener, Denis, in the crowd around a burning car, brandishing a knobkerrie. He had aimed away from Denis, but of course the others hadn't. Her nephew said that Barry, their officer, who was a nice boy, really, when you saw him at home, well, after the incident (that's what they called it), Barry turned the bodies over with the toe of his boot, keeping his gun almost touching them in case a wounded native attacked. Some unwary soldiers had been badly hurt when they knelt down to examine a body. . . . It was horrible. Her nephew said Barry flicked Smarties into his mouth with his left hand all the time he was turning the bodies over.

Patrick took no part in these conversations, and little in any others. He spent most of his time in the yard, where he was at first treated with sullen obstructiveness by the laborers. However, he persisted politely and they gradually thawed. He worked for hours with the native mechanic, learning how to dismantle and reassemble the filling machines. The mechanic called him Pat and shared his coffee.

One evening Mr. Mitchell took Patrick home to dinner and filled him with red wine, which unlocked what he had been keeping shut in. He described how a crowd of black children, teenagers and younger, came down a lane, jumping up and down, shouting, "Amandla! Amandla! Here are the Boers!" They seized one of Patrick's men, and when he, Patrick, ran towards them, two or three tires were thrown over his head, pinning his arms and legs. Several more tires followed, till he was like a Michelin advertisement. He was trapped, powerless, and could not see out. Around him the children were shouting, "A Boer, a Boer! Make a barbecue!" and were trying to light the tires with flaming newspapers. Then someone dispersed the children and pushed him over so that he could crawl out of the tires. He did not see who saved him; whoever it was had taken his tin hat as a trophy, no doubt to show Patrick that he could have killed him if he had wanted to.

"God, Mitch, I was scared. Shit scared. I'm still scared," Patrick confessed. "Can you imagine what it's like to be hated like that by a mob of kids you don't even know, and they've never seen you but they hate you? There's something wrong, man."

This was not all. When he got back to his men, he saw a black youth flat on his stomach, crawling along beside a wall, obviously trying to get to the rear of the soldiers. He was carrying a bottle, presumably full of gasoline, with a rag tied to it. Patrick shot him dead. "I didn't tell him to drop it, or call one of the chaps with a shotgun to pepper him with birdshot. That would have been enough. He was only a kid, Mitch, only twelve or thirteen. If it had happened in the Namib, if he was a Swapie, that would be different. He'd be our land's enemy, eh. But this kid, in Muzimuhle! I don't suppose the poor little bugger even understood what was going on." He shook his head. "I'm not sure I do, either."

Bonnie was still away. Mr. Mitchell sent the mechanic to her home, but her family knew nothing: she had gone to a funeral and had not returned. The hospitals had no record of her. The police refused to say whether they were holding her, but next day two Special Branch men — one white, one black — came to the plant and asked whether Bonnie had left anything behind. Papers, perhaps?

Their keys smoothly unlocked the drawer of Bonnie's desk. The black security man put aside a comb, lipstick, and aspirins, and carefully lifted out a small diary address book. A photo fell out of it: a seaside snap of Bonnie overflowing a bikini and bra. Across the bottom was written *Nigra sum sed formosa, eh? Bonnie.*

"Is it a code?" the black man asked.

"Hey, Mr. Mitchell, look here," the white official called. "Look, Latin."

Mr. Mitchell smiled perfunctorily. "We didn't do Latin at my school; we did geography instead."

"What does it say, chief?" the black man insisted.

"We had Latin right up to matric," the white official said. "Bloody boring, but useful. *Nigra sum,* I am black, *sed formosa,* but having shape. I am black but having shape. Can you beat that?"

"There's a piece in the Bible," Mr. Mitchell ventured, "I am black but comely, o ye daughters of Jerusalem. It's in the Song of Songs."

The Special Branch men looked at him with respect. "Would you say it again? It will score me a few points with the director. He's a great one for the Bible." He wrote the quotation in his notebook. "It would be useful to know who she intended it for."

"He will not need his Latin dictionary for a while, eh, chief," the black man said. "I am glad my girl has not schooled past standard four."

The two officials questioned Annie, Shirley, and Maxine separately about Bonnie's acquaintances, phone calls, and political opinions, but all that any of them could produce was that she talked about Jung as if he were a prophet, the way some people talked about the late Dr. Verwoerd, the creator of apartheid. No, it was Jung, sounding like *y-o-o-n-g,* not Yunif Abdul, the Cape Malay politician.

Before they left, the white Special Branch man had a private word with Mr. Mitchell: If anyone should inquire after Bonnie, which was improbable, would Mr. Mitchell please report it as a matter of urgency? Also, if he or the white staff could recall anything more regarding the race or whereabouts of this fellow Yoong . . .

Vilakazi returned soon afterwards, thinner and as taciturn as Patrick had been. He questioned the girls in detail about Bonnie and the Special Branch men, but when they asked what he thought — they were sure he would know something — he merely shook his head and muttered under his breath.

Mr. Mitchell pumped his hand and kept telling him how glad he was to see him, then pulled him into his private office and produced a jacket from the closet. "Better wear this," he said with exaggerated casualness. "You don't want people talking about those round Band-Aids on your chest. I can see them through your shirt. Shotgun pellets, eh?"

Vilakazi smiled guiltily and took the jacket.

Patrick waited for him in the main office. "Hi, V. Long time no see," he said, holding out his hand. Vilakazi ignored the hand and nodded curtly.

"Like to look over the works orders? We're running a bit behind schedule," Patrick said, opening the door to his office. He pulled up a chair for Vilakazi and brought his own chair round the table so that he and Vilakazi would be sitting side by side. Vilakazi picked up his chair and moved it back to the other side of the table. Patrick turned the pile of papers round so that they would be right side up for Vilakazi. "I can read upside down," Patrick volunteered apologetically. "I had a spell as apprentice draftsman when I left school."

Vilakazi said nothing but began perusing the papers. Patrick said hesitantly, "V, I wanted to tell you, I want you to know, I don't agree with what's going on. I don't like it at all."

Vilakazi continued reading a works order, moving his finger along a row of figures.

"They put me on duty in Muzimuhle, you know," Patrick went on.

"How many kaffirs did you get?" Vilakazi asked without looking up.

"Please don't talk like that, V man. I did kill someone. I shot a youngster, man, and I can't stop thinking about it. I've even prayed. I went to a church and prayed for forgiveness. But it makes no difference."

Vilakazi kept his finger on a column of figures. "You could try wearing one of these," he said sardonically, fingering his iziqu with his free hand. "But they won't help if it's forgiveness you want. Our spirits do not forgive."

"I keep thinking about that kid. He was only about the age of my young brother," Patrick said.

Vilakazi at last looked up. "Why are you so scared, or sad, or whatever it is, about one dead person? It's the living you should be worried about, man. Twenty million of us. Like Bonnie. And me."

"That's what I mean," Patrick responded eagerly. "I am worried. I'm against all this shooting. And I want you and me to be friends."

"That's nice to know." Vilakazi smiled without friendliness, picked up the works order he had been studying, and went out. A moment later he put his head in at the door and asked loudly, so that everyone in the office could hear, "Hey, Patrick, suppose that next time, when you are patrolling Muzimuhle in your Casspir, you see me standing square in the road in front of you. What will you do, man? How will you show that we are friends?"

He marched mock-soldierly into the yard and shouted unnecessary orders to the laborers.

Mr. Mitchell looked in at Patrick's office. "Try not to upset Vilakazi, old chap," he said. "It's a bad time for all of us."

"I only wanted to be friends again," Patrick protested. "I don't know what got into him. My unit doesn't even use Casspirs."

Pure Hamitic
Strain

◈

A FRONT TIRE went flat about two hours after we left
Johannesburg. We were on a stretch of road where there
was nothing but sparse thorn scrub. The last habitation
we had seen was six or seven miles back, and it was a
long time since we had passed another vehicle. A dusty,
red footpath crossed the road, apparently leading from
nowhere to nowhere. Along it stretched a line of termites,
each carrying a small burden. They followed the footpath
for a few feet, then veered into the scrub.

As soon as we stopped moving, the temperature in the
car rose to ninety.

According to the road map we were about six miles
from Qoqo, whatever that was. Even if it had a service
station, and even if the place was operating, that would
be no help. It would take me a couple of hours walk to
get there, and in any case I could not leave Mona alone
in the car. I was not very comfortable even about myself:
you never know what might happen in one of these god-
forsaken native areas nowadays.

When I was a boy I had assisted or watched dozens of times while a tire was being fixed. That was when tires still had inner tubes, which had to be patched with a patch and stuff called solution. One tested the valve by putting saliva on it: if it produced a little balloon, it was leaking. I knew about that, and about putting sand up against a tire while you pumped it so that you could see whether it was filling up and moving away from the sand. I did not have to do any of these things with this car, just take off one wheel and put on the spare — undo five nuts and do up five nuts — but whenever I tackle these jobs, something goes wrong and I hurt my hand or break some small, vital part of the machine.

"I'll have to change the wheel," I told Mona.

She took the car rug, her sunhat, and her paperback, skirted the procession of termites, and found a sliver of shade below an overhanging thorn shrub. "Have fun, darling," she said. "I do admire engineers and men who fix things. Call me if you want me to hold something while you spit on your hands."

The trunk was full of Mona's shapeless parcels. I had to take them all out to get to the tool kit and the spare wheel. They formed a multicolored mound on the road verge. The wheel spanner, thank God, fitted the nuts on the spare wheel. The nuts, however, would not move. I found a small rock that conveniently fitted my hand, and was about to start knocking the spanner when a respectful voice said, "Dag, baas." ("Dag" is Afrikaans for "Good day.")

The speaker was a tall, bare-chested African youth of fifteen or so. He wore clean khaki shorts, and sandals made from a tire, and carried two sticks of the kind the natives in these parts use as weapons. One stick is for hitting your opponent; the second is for warding off his blows.

I said, "Yah, boy," which is how you return the greeting, and wondered whether to ask him to stay and help. Even a dumb native would be useful to move things or pass tools or provide a bit of muscle, and this one looked quite intelligent.

He was also rather handsome, I noticed, and his skin was an unusual color — more like a heavy tan than the chocolate brown of the local Bantu.

"I help master," he volunteered.

"Yes, my boy, you help," I replied. "Master pay."

He reached into the trunk for my little rock and put it carefully on the road, took the wheel spanner from me, and effortlessly removed the nuts. Apparently I had been tightening them.

Mona raised herself on an elbow and watched with interest. "Someone knows more about cars than some people I know," she said.

The young man removed the wheel, rolled it down to the front of the car, and collected the jack and jack handle. He talked quietly and continuously to himself as he worked, occasionally frowning, smiling, or pulling a face.

"Good-looking specimen," Mona went on. "No thick lips or flat nose or anything Negroid. Copper skin. Pure Hamitic strain, Professor Schapera would say. Interesting throwback."

As he fitted the jack, the youth went on talking. When I came closer he stopped, but not before I had heard enough to recognize that he was speaking English. I with-

drew to the other side of the car and listened carefully.
He resumed his quiet monologue, talking in the slightly
haw-haw accent that some South African English-speakers
affect: " — real ladies' man, Eric Olsen . . . white or
black . . . pretty wife and two kids in Pretoria. . . . Out
here he couldn't pass an ntombi without giving her a
rub. . . handsome fellow, devil-may-care. . . . Little bastard is his spitting image . . . sort of kaffir Viking . . ."

He took off the flat wheel and fitted the spare, then
came round to the other side of the car.

"Baas put air?" He mimed an air hose. "Pssss?"

"No," I confessed. "I don't know."

He nodded understandingly and went back to the wheel,
again talking softly as he levered the jack. He had adopted
an Afrikaans accent. "Tough on a half-caste kid . . . Not
one thing nor the other. . . . That's why we need an
Immorality Act, eh. . . . Should make fellows like Olsen
live in the bloody native reserve. . . . If he wants a nigger
bitch, let him live like a nigger. . . ."

He came round and beckoned me to inspect the wheel.
It had remained mercifully plump. "Master lucky," he
commented.

"You're a good mechanic," I said.

"I try, master."

"What's your name, my boy?"

"I am Ishmael, master."

"Ishmael!" Mona broke in from the other side of the
car. "That was the son of Abraham's concubine. What
was her name? Hagar. Why would anyone give a kid a
name like that?"

He left us and began repacking the trunk. He stowed

the tool kit, fitted each of Mona's parcels neatly into a place where it would stay put, and placed my little rock carefully on the shoulder of the road. He whispered to himself in a precise, schoolmasterish voice, "A clever boy, very clever. If his father cared at all he would send him to a colored school where he would be with other mixed-blood children. . . . I believe he has never even seen the boy. . . . Doesn't care. . . . Paid the woman's father a few cows as compensation and that was it. . . ."

He closed the trunk and came and stood where I was folding Mona's rug. I gave him five rand. "Thank you, Ishmael. You did a wonderful job."

He held the money, native-style, in both hands. "Baas pay good. Like for white man. Not kaffir pay."

"Why do you talk like that? You can speak perfectly good English, can't you?"

He looked at me in surprise, then smiled a big, white-toothed smile, sharing a joke with us. "Good-looking specimen. Pure Hamitic strain, Professor Schapera would say." He exactly reproduced Mona's Cape accent and raised his voice at the end of the sentence, just as she did.

He picked up his sticks, gave us an African-style salute with high-raised palm — "Dag, baas, dag, missies" — and jogged up the footpath, slapping his sandals noisily against the earth and making little puffs of red dust as he went. He disappeared into the scrub in a few moments. We could hear him singing a loud, sad native song.

"Cheeky bastard," Mona said. "But competent. And very good-looking. He'd wow the women tourists on a Greek island. I wonder what will become of him?"